THE MERMAID'S TALE

SOPHIA DELAAT

Paper Wrights, LLC
www.paperwrights.co

Soulfulness is an apt description for the mermaid's quest.
.... the union of person and community, the masculine and feminine the word and the deed, the fairytale and the reality.

Sophia's depth and scope in describing literature, luminaries, destinations, life experiences, and world events across millennia is phenomenal.

Dr. Sharon Votel
Professor of Human Development
Saint Mary's University, Minneapolis, MN

For Rian and
in loving memory of Nina LaVern

Love is the triumph of imagination over intellect.
H.L. Mencken

Contents

PREFACE

An African proverb relates a sad truth:
When an elder dies, a library burns to the ground...

These words resound across cultures. Not only does the library burn down, but in today's society, a life well lived is seldom questioned, celebrated, or inspected. Even if the desire to share is present, can anyone answer a question not asked? As I approach my elder years I have chosen to share my story before my library burns down. What is this web of time and what makes living worth the struggle, especially if drugs, money, and sex do not capture your soul? A small still voice whispers to me, "Do not forget, do not forget, do not forget to remember." Bit by bit the tale of my life fits together. I am delighted to find upon inspection that I do have something to say.

Not to brag, but as a woman, I have endured the major initiations of surviving the 1950s, '"60s' and, etc. decades to face a patriarchy, unprepared to stand on my own two feet. My life has been a crash course majoring in physical and spiritual healing. I claim no innocence having been seduced and fallen prey to a multitude of sins. Disappointment has been my family's poison causing me to collapse in the face of failures. I have been homeless, a single mother, banished from my family, been reborn and resurrected to be patched together by prayer and grace only to be put back on the only path worth following; the practice of becoming a decent enough vessel to hold the precious substance of spirit.

The Mermaid's Tale proposes a perspective on becoming seen through the lens of sacred texts including myth and fairytale. These stories contain images of soul craft and transformation. They are not to be read, memorized to be test ready, quoting chapter and verse but are living stories we can recognize as we become the heroine in the journey towards autonomy and self-reliance.

When I used to read fairytales;
I fancied that kind of thing never happened
And here I am in the middle of one.
Lewis Carroll

Stories can be medicine that acts as a digestive agent akin to photosynthesis turning experience into wisdom. Robbed of this psychosynthesis (a new word for direct experience) the would-be initiate is tricked into believing truth can be read in a book. Truth is not simple or linear but conveyed as a story to be lived. It is often paradoxical requiring the reconciliation of opposites, solving a conundrum or koan. The reward is the great A HA! that accompanies enlightenment. Albert Einstein would agree with me as he too championed the worthiness of fairy tales.

If you want your children to be intelligent,
Read them fairy tales.
If you want them to be more intelligent,
Read them more fairy tales.

Certainly, tales are multinational and are also interrupted on different levels of understanding of the human condition. Freud, Rudolf Steiner, Carl Jung, and Wolfgang Goethe would also agree with me that fairy tales nurture the dream life and feed the imagination. Symbols or archetypes assist the psyche in negotiating the waking consciousness. My 22 years as a Waldorf teacher taught me how desperate is the need for not only the young child to experience stories and fairy tales, but also the adult. These imaginations of transformation reach into the deepest recesses of the body, mind, and will to foster creativity, the elixir of becoming more truly human.

I had no idea what I would discover when I started *on The Mermaid's Tale*. The longer I sat with each question, the more I realized to what extent the feminine aspect of humanity has been amputated from history. Amputated may sound like a harsh word for the veiling, shrouding, and circumcision of women in order that any man's head not be turned to seduction. I believe attraction is so extreme that the men of history have had to overpower and control the object of desire. Women are not innocent in this tragedy. Everyone uses what power they may have to get what they want. What we read in so many tales are that it is now time for men and women to take control of history and redeem the kingdom. Learning to ride a horse, play an instrument, or carve a gourd requires the would-be artist to know the rules of engagement and the language of the discipline. Language is so important, especially today when words can take on different meanings. Symbols and archetypes stem from a meaning much deeper than individual perception. Learning the world of stories requires further study. They can be our daily bread.

The Brothers Grimm are responsible for the greater work of recording a treasury of stories that led to the study of folklore. Stories like *Mother Holle*, a Grimm's tale, reward those who meet everyday tasks with joy and diligence. The Italian tale of *The Three Oranges* warns that the solution to a problem may be presented by the least suspecting intruder on the journey. Another Grimm's story, *Rumplestilkin* tells us that knowing the secret name of things reveals that straw can be spun into gold. Perhaps this world is more supernatural than we have been educated to believe.

I have, however, chosen three tales for *The Mermaid's Tale* to point to a tender birthing of the feminine soul that is much more than women's liberation. The time has come for the reclaiming of the kingdom lost in the pursuit of money and power. It is time to reclaim the pursuit of the beautiful, to engage in art, and care for the earth as the original mandate for life on this planet. This is the threshold of the SHIFT in consciousness when the unseen values of compassion and integrity are honored as much if not more than the bottom line. These tales have been my tales, but they are also the story of our collective soul as we approach a flowering plane of self-discovery. Nature has her story as well. In the language Goethe may have used, a plant yearns for the light. The flowering process is a part of the plant's yearning to becoming more, so much more that some plants have learned to produce fruit. The plant's activity is interesting enough to connect to the next kingdoms of birds and bees. If interesting enough, human creativity can be the elixir to connect to the next kingdom as well - The Angelic Kingdom.

If we as a species have forgotten how to connect, then dreaming, learning the language of symbol and archetype, and seeking the love of the deed are connecting and remembering that life is a gift of discovery.

Teach me to hear the mermaid's singing.
John Donne

PROLOGUE

This passage from Ecclesiastics 1:9 has gone undisputed for thousands of years, and for those thousands of years, human beings have been assembling and deconstructing these multiple expressions of a Supreme Unknown. The enigma of what is a human being is equally challenging, especially when we move beyond the notion that a human being is incidental as a determining factor in earthly evolution. In his novel, *Stranger In a Strange Land*, Robert Heinlein labeled attempts at arriving at basic Truths: to Grok. Grok describes intelligence at work as thought: interpreting, synthesizing, and extrapolating impressions in an attempt to decode the essence of the moment. Miraculously, astute questioning leads to answers that seem to fit together in ever-expanding patterns, much like the self-replicating pentagrams.

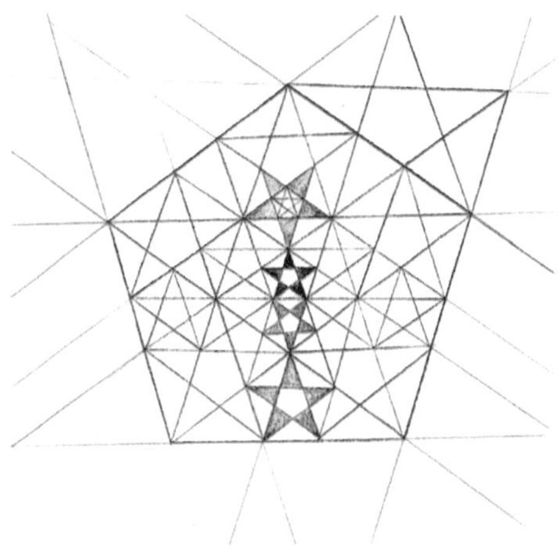

There was a time in the not-so-distant past when families held most of the community's population in a congruent interpretation of its Truth. Boys were initiated into the family business, guild, or farm at an early age, and girls seldom questioned that their lives would differ very much from their mothers'. Those days of following in the footsteps of a family member have been abandoned. There are now precious few absolute truths or leaders to show the way. Tragically our young are now left to their own devices to create meaning from life's trials and tribulations.

The resulting dissonance obscures emerging patterns, inhibiting the best of us from being able to *grok* personal revelation. That being said, I have experienced the *great nothing* and come to some theories of my own. I have traveled extensively and have lived in more places than I can recount; each move, no matter how far, was another beginning. I have become practiced in the reconstruction of my life and am familiar enough with the process to determine what is essential. This rolling stone has been broken and repaired but has gathered little moss.

Many philosophers, thinkers, and tinkers of the world have influenced me, but Rudolf Steiner and Wolfgang von Goethe have inspired me to love what I do and trust the silent voice of personal revelation. My initiations, however, have not been at the feet of great masters, but by children and through fairy tales. I thank innumerable children who have given me grace and allowed me into their world of wonder where there is the possibility of joy, imagination, and creativity. To know this possibility has been remarkable.

Symbolically, a circle illustrates the intimate connection to everything that the child naturally has prior to, oddly enough, the change of teeth. The lack of what an adult would call judgment allows impressions direct access to the slumbering soul. A child orders these chaotic sense experiences to form the basic constructs of her worldview. However, this tender time of childhood is threatened today.

Young children are rushed to decisions without the benefit of experience on which to base an opinion as simple as whether or not they prefer soda or milk. Indecisive parents look to their children for clues for bedtime, what to fix for dinner, or even what to buy at the grocery store. It is as if adults fear the authority to know what a human being requires to develop the gifts and talents this world so dearly needs. The lack of meaningful rhythm, early intellectualization, and exposure to technology have arrested the child's natural ability to play. A part of the young heart becomes frozen by predetermined concepts.

> *Human beings are only fully human when they play,*
> *and they only play when they are human*
> *in the fullest sense of the word.*
> *—Schiller, poet of freedom*

Children test moment to moment just to find out what we are made of. They have taught me that no matter what the curriculum, we (teachers and parents) not only teach who we are, but who we aspire to be; we teach our intentions. This is what children want to know first and foremost. Any arbitrary use of authority or power to gain access or control of them is met with a variety of resistances. These assaults on childhood break down the dream, a natural protection of childhood. The greatest gift a child can receive is to gently wake from this dream so that imagination and intelligence can meld into living thinking. From out of the circle, the unique individuality emerges to master left-right orientation or linear capacities.

Fairy tales are written in the language of pictures and with every telling, a tale can take on a new significance. This is the language of the dream where everyone is everything. Dreams are where we go to make sense of the world we encounter in the harsh light of day. In the land of the fairy tale, pearls are mermaid's tears. Pearls are created by a minor irritation out of which, over time, the oyster creates a valuable treasure. Gratefully I have transformed little and large irritants into pearls of varying degrees of perfection. *The Mermaid's Tale* is how I have strung these pearls of experience into something of value. Surely, nothing less will do, as this is the very foundation on which individual freedom is built.

> *Whosoever survives a test, whatever it may be,*
> *must tell the story. That's his (her) duty.*
> *—Elie Wiesel, 1986 Nobel Peace Prize winner*

Free, living thought is the evolutionary goal of spiritual development. *The Mermaid's Tale* is not meant to be an absolute Truth, but these are my thoughts, my Truth, and the best representation of the Truth that has led to an intimate conversation with the powers that create me. One Truth I will hold fast to is that in any circumstance, we have the choice to enjoy the ride or not. Simply said, it is best to choose to enjoy it. Charnie Lewis, my favorite riding instructor, told me, "Smile, your horse knows if you are enjoying the ride!" I have found this to be the best advice in any circumstance.

The writing of *The Mermaid's Tale* has given heart to my experience—so much so that I highly recommend the process to anyone over sixty, or with enough life experience to have wisdom based on personal "ahas" and revelations. I am interested in thinking that redefines established premises. These thoughts don't have to be magnificent revelations that challenge a world order like whether or not the earth is round or flat, Galileo's confrontation with the Catholic Church, or the Declaration of Independence that established the value of freedom. What I find most interesting is not research filled with statistics, but in how personal limitations have been creatively redefined. Every victory towards independence, from learning to walk through developmental stages that mark the emerging self is a reason for celebration. How a person becomes real is a matter that should concern all of us.

Some friends are able to shine through life, even making the daily grind look effortless, while others of us wrestle with our demons to learn the sacred arts of becoming. I am thankful for the former because they keep the world in balance while others of us tinker around with basic premises guided by a desire to taste the elixir called Life, reverently served in the most beautiful of chalices: our earth, community, and the living Grail of our own beings.

Once you are Real you can't become unreal again.
It lasts for always.
—Margery Williams, the Velveteen Rabbit

CHAPTER 1

Nothing Is Small

Yes, indeed, there is a Santa Claus. There are princesses and wicked stepmothers, kings, and queens, and they all inhabit a world known to many as the Middle Kingdom. These are the cast of characters of the imagination and subconscious. They are remnants and memories from our collective childhoods when eternity was traded in for the experience of Time. Since this forgetting, the human race has turned its gaze ever outward toward adventures of personal invention. These stories have been abandoned or reinterpreted, and the Middle Kingdom has faded from view. Sigmund Freud, Carl Jung, and Rudolf Steiner, to name a few, reveal the story behind these tales. Each rendition is different, each true from its perspective. At whatever level of awareness, understanding is granted to all believers in perseverance, magic, the power of intention, and the grace of a pure heart. Within these stories is the world of God's creative power. This world exists where Life issues forth, mediating heaven and earth. It is also known as the Land of Heart's Desire. Many a prince has tried to pass the thorny hedge or sought the Waters of Life only to get lost in searching. It is a perilous endeavor with few guarantees.

What is essential to the heart is invisible to the eye.
—The Fox to the Little Prince

Fortunately, it is a world guarded by virtue, as only the heart may find it. The natural citizens of this land, at the periphery of our understanding, serve as a bridge between the worlds and participate in the vital process of Nature. This Middle Kingdom is a place where Life enchants all it touches. The workforce consists of the elementals: earth, fire, air, and water as represented in story form as gnomes, undines, salamanders, and sylphs. They are respected as those who convey Life through the realms of Nature. Technology and the extreme intellectualism of the Western world have eclipsed our understanding of what we cannot see with our eyes. In the past, human beings went to extremes to attract the attention, aid, and assistance of the unseen. All indigenous cultures hold dear to these little folk, by different names, because they were keenly aware that the happiness of the elemental life ensured a blessing from this enchanted realm. This world holds the secrets of creation, transformation, and regeneration. Unrecognized and unheeded, these powerful forces invade human nature, causing us to lose our balance and push the reckless to excesses or one-sidedness. As per the NASA website, the human eye is limited to what it can see of the electromagnetic spectrum. The spectrum includes red, orange, yellow, green, blue indigo, and violet, but this is just a fraction of what is actually going on around us.

There is nothing so secular that it cannot be sacred,
and that is one of the deepest messages of the Incarnation.
—Madeleine L'Engle

Personal effort and sacrifice are now demanded to assuage Nature and the angels who have lost interest in our human plight. These forces of creation have withdrawn their influence so that we become more involved in the evolution of planet Earth. To attract their attention, we have to cultivate a feeling of life in order to perceive this subtle world. Out of respect for individual freedom, no hand of the invisible will interfere unless invited. Then and only then will they willingly join forces with us in the service of evolution.

Saint Paul taught that we live life prayerfully. He did not mean that we recite a continuous loop of the Lord's Prayer, but that we become mindful of the effects our thoughts and deeds have on the sensitive, alert world we share with a host of creative spirits. Because our imagination is so limited, we must develop a vocabulary of symbols that facilitates an active imagination regarding the forces that create our reality. Perhaps then, our words and meditations would make us worthy of partnership with the unseen.

> *In our era, the road to holiness*
> *passes through the world of action.*
> —*Dag Hammarskjold,*

It therefore behooves us to get to know these architects of creation, these magicians of form. We owe them our gratitude as it is their labor that animates the natural world. Their life is the life of becoming and transformation. How does a mountain grow? How does a drop of water survive time to transform itself and the geography it interacts with? Observe the gentle transformation through daybreak or the persistent and relentless river's rush to the sea to appreciate the creative forces of Nature. What genius is at work that causes rain to fall from the sky or bows a rainbow across the horizon? If not beings of conscious awareness, gnomes, undines, sprites, and sylphs exhibit personality in the way they interact to create the world.

This symphony of forces orchestrates the miraculous. The Middle Kingdom is not static, but alive and capable of relationship. It is intelligent with a sense of humor, but shy in the face of disbelief.

Infinite riches are all around you if you will open your mental eyes and behold the treasure house of infinity within you.
There is a gold mine within you from which you can extract everything you need to live life gloriously, joyously, and abundantly.
—Joseph Murphy

Marjorie Spock, also a student of Rudolf Steiner, has studied this kingdom and assures us that it is possible to go beyond the prison of the mundane physical world to learn the language of this invisible realm. She wrote poetically about all the inhabitants of the Middle Kingdom, about their habits and gestures. She relates that these beings are not flesh and blood, but have bodies formed of the light stuff of intelligence as they are the intelligence of Nature. I am most grateful for her study and authorship, for much of the following I have gleaned from her writing.

Every blade of grass has an angel that bends over it and whispers grow, grow!
—The Talmud

GNOMES

Gnomes are the ancient race of elementals closest to our understanding. Without them there would be no solid ground, no firm bodies or bones, and no logical structure to our thinking. They are the formative force in earthly substance, and they see ideas as we see objects. Gnomes don't have to figure anything out, they just know. They are awake to the environment, sensitive to our thoughts and feelings, and they never sleep. These industrious creatures marshal nutrients to plants wield magnetic forces, and love order. They are mischievous and love to poke and prod the unsuspecting human beings who fancy themself above mistake. Humans see the world as unchanging; gnomes see it as moving forces endowed with music. Their love of knowledge is like a magnet attracting thoughts that flow into evolution from the mind of God.

Because wisdom does not necessarily proceed in a linear fashion, let us consider here that the elemental world is a world that exists parallel and reciprocally to the world of humankind. The elemental world is one of processes: changing, becoming, disappearing, and manifesting. Life and death are perceptible forces that reveal infinite possibilities and variations on similar themes.

Nature allows the inquisitive to look at the process from every direction. This world defies gravity and is therefore not bound by the same reasoning and laws of Third Dimensional reality. It is not too much of a stretch to think of the world we live in as a living, breathing being. Tides roll in and out, and day breaks and the sun sets as rhythmically as a beating heart. For the casual observer, winter appears as though a great sleep has fallen across the land. But, if one were to question where all the life that supported leaf and fruit has gone, there is but one conclusion. Sap and seed have been called home. Deep in the earth, Nature is getting ready for the next cycle. The earth herself is most awake in the winter. In spring, Mother Earth breathes out, but no flower could bloom without the careful preparations that took place in the winter. After her work is complete, and set in motion, Nature begins her rest. To this end, we enjoy her dreaming in the summer.

At first, this may feel counterintuitive, but reflect on the personal experience of winter. We are more introspective, and more inwardly awake during the winter months. Summer may be more playful, but without the reflection and preparation of the winter, we would not have the consciousness we need to fully grasp the complexities of the modern world. Winter is the season of the gnome, when all of summer's activity is called home and the earth is the most awake.

When our lives become chaotic, and we become hypnotized into believing that the material world is all there is, these elemental forces invade human thinking, shriveling true thinking to cold logic. It is then easy to forget the redemptive power of the arts and nature. We can be tricked into believing that what we see is all there is. I know from firsthand experience that the gnomes in my home are more content when order prevails, clutter is banished, and the floors are swept of dust and cat hair. I have found lost keys in just the place I had looked for them. It is as if a gnome had been sitting upon them the whole time! Playful, yes. Irritating? Absolutely. Kindergarten teachers I know will testify that the gnomes in their classrooms pinch and aggravate the children if the classroom has not been loved and tidied. Even the quality of sound in an ordered room is enhanced when everything has been touched and put in its place. Gnomes, and therefore human beings, are content in a room that is kept in order.

UNDINES

When we turn our attention to the watery realm of the undine, we have to abandon a sharp focus in favor of the more fluid element of liquid dreaming mixed in a sea of images. The experience is more a feeling than gnome thinking. Undines are the Great Transformers; they are the chemists of the elemental world, where water and air commingle. Water is a creative force that expresses itself as dew, rain, snow, and sleet. It is expansive, violent, and destructive. Water is immortal; it is part of the trilogy of life: sunlight, oxygen, and water. Our planet is, in fact, defined by water.

The undine is in the flowing of dew and sap in trees. Undines come into being and then dissolve into clouds and mists, ever expanding, and contracting. Spring is their favorite season, when they join with the upward flow of Nature's dreaming. Without undines, there would be no life-giving oceans, streams, or green vegetation. A world without undines would be a world devoid of feeling in our soul or purpose in our living. These creatures are protectors of sacred springs and are found in forest pools and waterfalls where their beautiful voices can be heard in the splashing water. Names for water elementals are undine, kelpie, wraith, naiad, siren, and mermaid.

The Thunder releases the water, and the water is medicine for everything. Water is the medicine of Creation. The Thunder roars and makes people frightened, but it brings the rains that purify and nourish everything. So bring us your Thunder, so the Rains will come.
—Flaming Rainbow Woman

In 1999, a Japanese researcher by the name of Masau Emoto published *Message from Water*. His work appeared in the movie *What the Bleep Do We Know?* I heard his presentation at an elementary school in Los Angeles. He shared his research with these young people because he understood the important implications of his work. Emoto's premise is that human thought and emotion have the power to affect the structural patterns of water at the molecular level. Higher thoughts and feelings have subtle vibrations that create pristine patterns as the water molecules are frozen into snowflakes. These snowflakes are clearly more beautiful than molecules exposed to lower vibratory levels of disgust, envy, rage, or hate. The implication of responsibility for our thoughts is made obvious through his research that redefines the nature of water as a substance that has memory and can carry consciousness right down to the molecular level.

SPRITES

The fire elementals are called salamanders or sprites. Without them, there would be no warmth, no hearth, no fruit, fragrance, or grain. There would be no fire-core of selfhood. In the extreme fiery invasion, a human being even appears puffed up when filled with fiery self-importance. The sprite weaves cosmic warmth into cosmic love and tends the spark in the seed that the gnomes nourish throughout the winter. The warmth/fire element in oils is responsible for the ripening fruit and the inner world of visions that fuel evolution.

Only recently have the advances in photography allowed science to confirm the presence of high-altitude flashes that take place above thunderstorms? Scientists have known that high in the troposphere, and well above the turbulent parts of the atmosphere, ultraviolet rays from the sun strike gas molecules, knocking electrons loose to form the ionosphere. This is an electrically conductive layer around the earth. With high-speed photography, they are now able to confirm what high-flying pilots suspected, but could not prove. Two types of high-level lightning are now called *sprites and elves*. Researchers are not in agreement about what these extraterrestrial phenomena represent. Scientists remain in a state of awe and wonder when they behold these bursts of energy that "dance through the ethereal world between earth and space."

SYLPHS

Sylphs are bodiless beings who are ever-present in the movement of air. The structural similarities between a leaf and a feather may give the more poetic reader pause to wonder about the architects of such fine work. The forms are unmistakably generated by the same shaping energy. The air itself has substance, if we could but see it. The air is a parallel realm where sound travels, birds migrate, and insects make their way from flower to flower. It is a world of tone, where sylph flight makes music. The air is latticed with the glittering, streaking paths of these small meteors. We breathe in this air that has been imbued with musical force! Autumn is the natural season of sylphs when Nature turns inward. When an imbalance of the airy element is experienced by a human counterpart, the human tends to express itself in fanaticism.

Ernst Chladni was a nineteenth-century German physicist and musician who is considered the Father of Acoustics. The following experiment is one he used to demonstrate two- dimensional vibrations. I performed the following experiment as a part of a sixth-grade acoustics class. The experiment called for a cello bow, and a flat metal plate named after Chladni himself. First, we secured the Chladni plate, sprinkled salt on the plate, and I then bowed the plate with a cello bow-much like one might play a cello. Well bowed, and seemingly miraculously, the salt arranged itself according to specific notes or vibrations. Vibrations that lacked the integrity of a specific frequency would not create beautiful patterns, but with a little practice, the following patterns might appear. Sound creates a measurable impact, even if we cannot see it with our physical eyes.

The following table illustrates these mysterious patterns.

GOBLINS AND TROLLS

There is also the realm of the not-so-friendly elementals who add to the drama of nature. Sometimes called gremlins or goblins, they are behind the sting of poison. They ride in whirlwinds, summon volcanoes, and call down lightning. They are an aspect of the living soul of Nature where we experience earthquakes and landslides. Unsurprisingly, these tricksters lack social ability.

The real mystery of life is not a problem to be solved,
it is a reality to be experienced.
J.J. Van der Leeuw

NATURE'S INTELLIGENCE

Our biggest failure is our failure to see patterns.
Marilyn Ferguson

The intelligence pervading Nature is rapidly being reevaluated. With heartfelt observation, researchers are gaining access to a world of beauty and seduction. Fairytales describe this presence in Nature that conspires to deliver the protagonist from failure, release the kingdom from enchantment, and restore all to a higher order. The shift may seem to magically occur, but not without proper preparation. Rocks do not just decide when to turn to dust or roll away. The stone is at the mercy of fire, water, and wind. Geological change can happen in moments, but most often it is so slow that the human eye can be deceived into believing what is and always will be.

But, across the threshold into the plant kingdom, we enter a world of intrigue; a world of glamour where the elementals weave together to create life. Here the stars have petals in multiples of 2, 3, 5, 8, and 13. Though relatively new to evolution, these divas have refined the art of seduction to guarantee their species does not lose its place in the evolutionary scheme of things. In a relatively short period of time, 250,000 species of flowers have evolved; each species with a fingerprint so unique that elaborate rituals of propagation are imprinted within the plant kingdom and extend into the next insect to keep the intrigue going. Ah! Bewitching beauty and sweet nectar that lures the winged ones, again and again, to return for yet another sip. If we could observe the ritual or take pleasure in its genius we would most certainly be drunk with delight.

Some flowers may be discreet, but others are nothing short of promiscuous, spreading pollen all over the neighborhood or seeds cleverly transported, even across oceans. Carried by the wind, buried in the soil, or scorched to open-seeds have a remarkable endurance for the mission. Nature uses every means at her disposal; she has devised clever adaptations to procreate, even enlisting parasites, predation, and mimicry. It appears that consciousness is everywhere and in everything. Gnomes, sprites, sylphs, and undines may be characters in children's stories, but they are also vital forces that drive, balance, and sustain this planet. They are what weave together and create circumstances for Life.

When we seek for connection, we restore the world to wholeness. Our seemingly separate lives become meaningful as we discover how truly necessary, we are to each other. The divine circulations never rest nor linger. Nature is the incarnation of thought, and turns to a thought again, as ice becomes water and gas. The World is mind precipitated, and the volatile essence is forever escaping again into the state of free thought.
~ Ralph Waldo Emerson

THE HOLY GRAIL

Throughout European mythology, there are stories of a cauldron, chalice, or cup that predates Parzival's quest, or King Arthur and his Round Table. Cerridwen's cauldron was a vessel of wisdom and rebirth while another vessel satisfied all who came in need. It could feed, give drink, heal, and restore life. The cauldron was fired by the breath of the muses or brewed enough that no one would ever go hungry. None, that is, save the coward's share. In all cases the cauldron was associated with magic and otherworldliness; it may be guarded by a man, but always associated with the Feminine. In Ireland and Wales the pagan year was celebrated with festivals and songs to assure the blessings and perfection of what was above in the heavens would manifest on earth. There is considerable evidence that can lead one to believe that all the cup, cauldron, and grail legends have a common story to tell. Today the Grail continues to be a symbol of spiritual abundance wherein the community's integrity and relationship to nature determines its health, wealth, and well- being.

What is the Grail and where is it to be found have been the inspiration for stories and songs since Chrétien de Troyes inspired troubadours in the 1800s. There are many permutations of the story. The literal Holy Grail refers to the chalice that Jesus blessed during the Last Supper. The legend goes on to tell how Joseph of Arimethima caught the blood that flowed from Jesus at the crucifixion. Joseph journeyed west to the British Isles where he hid the chalice in a well. Today he is considered the original Guardian of the Grail.

In de Troyes' poem, Parzival is the original seeker of the Grail. His name means one who pierces the valley or one who passes safely between looming mountains. He visits the Grail Castle but lacks the spiritual maturity to ask the question that can heal Amfortas, the Grail king. Later versions connect stories of King Arthur and his Round Table to this quest, but make Galahad the seeker. Over time, the legend has evolved to make this quest synonymous with the transformation of the human being into the chalice of the Holy Spirit. This transformation demands both individual and spiritual responsibility.

Joseph Campbell and Robert Sardello, among others, consider this legend of the search for spiritual revelation as the founding myth of Western civilization. The stories are a prophecy of the future rather than a retelling of past occurrences. In them, the earthly experience is the initiation of individual Self-hood found not in perfection, but in learning from our imperfections to arrive at the right perspective of Self and community in which God evolves and evil is redefined. Through trials, one must prove oneself worthy of God's grace which is available to all who prepare.

The legend reveals an intimacy between the ways of Nature and the course of human destiny that is an unbreakable bond. Initiation is realized through an understanding that for every step taken in understanding the mysteries of this world, we must bring our actions into accord with our ideals by demanding of ourselves two steps in practical, willing execution. The time for only thinking nice thoughts or reading about spiritual development is over; the path to the future and fulfillment runs right through worldly and human involvement. We all know the way, or at least have read about it, but few make the effort to apply what we already know.

ALCHEMY

The practice of alchemy spanned three continents over four millennia; it dates back to a time when the species first began tinkering with earthly phenomena. At the pre-dawn of rational thought, where intelligence met mythologies, great minds developed theories of how the universe functioned based on the only tool available: observation. Alchemy is a proto-science that sprung from human curiosity to know how matter came into being. How does order come out of chaos? How does one create circumstances for the best to come to pass? Alchemy is the precursor of modern science where science became the systematic ordering of thoughts, the art of perceiving. The early alchemist sought to perceive the archetype in the transitory in order to find what was hidden. Hermes, the god of playful connections, was believed to be the bearer of this art that dealt creatively with limitation as the prima material, the point of departure of understanding how substance interacts in the world.

Today we look to the works of Aristotle as providing the founding thoughts for this investigation into the cloaked meaning of phenomena. Aristotle believed that the entire universe, the universal essence, was made up of a single formless substance that became the four elements: earth, air, fire, and water. The early alchemists believed harmony and musical proportion could be created merely by changing the balance of elements in a process called transmutation. By condensing and reconstituting, he and his students believed that circumstances could be created to remove any hindrance to development; through the process, base metals could be transformed into the noble metals of gold and silver. Gold was seen as the most perfect of metals, so much so that all metals were aspiring to become this perfection. They believed in strict observation and imitation of Nature as a foundation for thought. The works of Aristotle flourished throughout the Mediterranean and were carried further by Alexander the Great.

Alchemists had definitive objectives in mind. Two of the best known are the creation of the *philosopher's stone* that would change base metals into the noble metals of gold and silver, and the creation of the elixir of Life that conferred youth and immortality. If lesser metals could be transformed into higher metals, then it stood to reason that there was also a metaphysical component for those who sought to change the baser soul qualities into the more refined attributes of spirit. The entire philosophy revolved around their belief that the human soul was divided within itself after the Fall. Through purification, the soul could be reunited once again with God.

If you do not know essence and don't know Life, you will split the creative and receptive into two paths. But the day you join them together to form the elixir, you fall drunken into the jug yet have no need of support.
—Tan Guangzhen, Chinese philosopher

Plato, Aristotle, Paracelsus, Roger Bacon, Tycho Brahe, and one of the greatest geniuses of all time, Sir Isaac Newton, were great men who were associated with this Hermetic art. But, alchemy as an art fell into disrepute with the advent of rational materialism, and, of course, fantastic claims by charlatans. As a science of symbols and transformation, it lives on today in sophisticated circles of thought. Those who work closely with Nature are perhaps the purest alchemists. Farmers are by necessity alchemists who study and nurture the elemental life that is alive in the soil, water, and air to bring forth food filled with ethereal life and spirit. But in essence, all of us who are on the path of revelation are to some degree alchemists in that we seek the wisdom that allows the best to come to pass. Modern-day alchemists seek the harmony of divine proportion based on the transformative forces in Nature to heal themselves and their communities on both local and global levels.

All things are tied together. When you cut a tree, whose roots connect with everything, you must ask its forgiveness, or a star will fall out of the sky.
—*Lacandon Mayan proverb*

ROYAL ARCHETYPES

The royals of this realm are archetypes of human experience. Carl Jung wrote that the subconscious has a vast resource of archetypes that are the driving forces behind phenomena. An archetype is a universally understood symbol, image, or ideal example of an unconscious idea. There is an original theme and all the other expressions are mere variations. Simplistically, there is an archetype of a chair that all chairs share in varying degrees. Accordingly, male and female are human archetypes that are expressed as individual men and women. To come to an understanding of an archetype, one may ask, "What is essence?" Understanding archetypes helps to explain why the sea has been associated with the emergence of human consciousness from the oceans of the world. Our blood shares a similar saline composition as the sea, and our bodies have a similar ratio of water to earthy material, approximately 70 percent water. Life for us all begins in the oceanic waters of a mother's womb connecting us to the realm of fishes, dreams, and mythology. Cultures are created by shared experiences of archetypes that define society or a paradigm. A paradigm reflects the culture and creates institutions that hold the psychic fabric of the culture harmoniously together.

Fairy tales are stories of prophecy imbued with archetypes. They are stories that inform the sleeping part of us about the trials of becoming a human being. The old passes away and a new world begins. This storyline sounds ominously like the demise of the world paradigm based on an unhealthy hierarchical authority and the military regimes that we are witnessing today. And, thank goodness, these stories promise a new kingdom will emerge because of an integration of the archetypes of male and female that creates the authentic Self.

By and large, the king of the land is pretty dysfunctional. He is either old, in need of healing, lacking a queen, or non- existent. The old king's rule lacks authentic authority. Perhaps he lacks vision. He keeps order by carrying a big stick or has such a bad temper that his subjects comply. The stories build anticipation for the king-in-waiting, or the prince, to develop the necessary maturity to find his kingdom. The new king knows that compassionate endurance prevails where force cannot reach; healing the kingdom requires the awakening of the sleeping soul, the Feminine, who provides compassion for an authentic authority. The new king and queen join together to create a unified vision or new kingdom.

The new queen will not be shallow, petty, jealous, or manipulative. She will be a true mother who nurtures her children. Her wisdom flows from a heart that knows the mind to be a powerful ally, but not the dictator. In the case of the Grail King, Amfortas is without a queen. As a result, he has a wound that will not heal. His kingdom is in jeopardy, the people quarrel, fields lay barren, and cows do not give milk. The king is powerless and impotent without his Feminine counterpart. His kingdom is a stricken wasteland that will only be made whole when the Grail is restored. Unfortunately, today, the Grail has become a cliché for the sought-after excellence of product or performance; sought, but never found.

On a biological level, the left side of the brain is the kingside. The left side is primarily detail-oriented, and logical, has sequential perception, and is rational and precise. The right side, or the queen's side, thinks imaginatively in visual patterns but doesn't have verbal functions. The right side of the brain stores memory receives intuitive impressions, and experiences emotions. The sense of music resides deeply on the right side of the brain, so protected that when all other human faculties fail, music survives. The king is the archetype for thinking while the queen's forces reside deep in the sleeping, or unconscious will. The masculine, rational mind has, for good or for ill, acted for hundreds of years as the king. The slumbering princess is the awakening Feminine who will unite with the prince as the new queen to create the archetypical human to rule over an invigorated kingdom.

The princess inevitably is the central character in the tales of Becoming. The resolution takes place and the kingdom is restored when the Feminine awakens to take her rightful place in the order of creation to which she gives the personal feeling of the Self. Where the fairy tale ends, our future begins. The shift in consciousness taking place today requires us to have a fuller experience of the conversation between the Masculine and the Feminine, the king and queen, and the right and left sides of our brain. It is this conversation that evokes the vibrational matrix of the Kingdom. Connecting the brain's two hemispheres is the corpus callosum.

When both hemispheres are actively participating, thinking is informed by an experiential feeling and then elevated to inspiration, intuition, and imagination. Now the rulers know the details and have an imagination as to how to ascribe relevance to individual experience because information comes from a direct understanding of the needs and nature of the kingdom. The rulers grasp concepts without words because the left side understands what the right side is feeling.

The wicked stepmother is an archetype that often defines a fairytale. This stepmother is alive and well in every culture. While not every stepmother fits the script of the wicked queen, parenting is complicated. Mothering is an art that requires an expansion of soul-force and awareness that does not come naturally anymore. The future is dependent on parenting as a sacred calling.

Every character in a fairy tale is an expression of some aspect of the human psyche. We are each king and queen, wicked queen, prince and princess. Our soul is waking up through the living experience of the world. On the journey of self-discovery, we each have a story that is living through us and one we project out onto others. Disney has done an injustice to the human psyche by altering the plot lines to lead us to believe that the story is external and that a woman's salvation is achieved in marriage to a fantastic prince. We wait and wait to be disappointed when all we find is a mere mortal. We waste so much time without knowing that our salvation is as near as our own soul.

The human heart can go to the lengths of God.
Dark and cold we may be, but this
is no winter now. The frozen misery of centuries breaks, cracks,
begins to move,
the thunder is the thunder of the flows,
the thaw, the flood, the upstart Spring.
Thank God our time is now when wrong
comes up to face us everywhere
Never to leave us till we take
The longest stride of soul (we) ever took.
Affairs are now soul size.
The enterprise is exploration into God.
Where are you making for?
It takes so many thousand years to wake,
But will you wake for pity sake?
—from "A Sleep of Prisoners"
by Christopher Fry

The last verse of the Hebrew Bible reads:

Behold, I will send you Elijah the prophet
before the coming of the great and dreadful day of the Lord:
And he shall turn the heart of the fathers to the children
and the heart of the children to their fathers,
lest I come and smite the earth with a curse.
—Malachi 4:5

Every day a new subject line enters my email inbox announcing that humanity is undergoing a significant shift in consciousness. Subject lines offer emotional freedom, ways to liberate myself, and promises of feminine power and cash flow. A revolution is taking place and it is even being televised. The people of the world are demanding change. The grievances in Syria, Egypt, Greece, Chili, and Russia are not that different from the representatives of the ninety-nine percent of Americans who have gathered on Wall Street, and across the country on Main Street. The much-talked-about Shift is taking place, and change is everywhere—economically, spiritually, and politically. The institutions that held together the Piscean Age paradigm are disintegrating to make way for a New World. How the world experiences this freed energy is in witnessing its rush across TV screens with pictures of cultures in upheaval, and through our households with gale-force winds, literally destroying the past and taking with it dreams for the future and 401Ks. It is as if the very foundations of the world are changing. The stock market is erratic. Cities are in crisis. Mother Nature trembles and rolls as volcanoes erupt, fault lines move, and glaciers break off to float out to sea. Some days it feels as if we are adrift, like the iceberg, on a sea of change. Everywhere I look there is discontent. There is precious little leadership strong enough to harness this chaotic energy, or to bring communities together in a shared purpose with a living vision of how to effect positive change. What is changing? What is staying the same? What is the emerging wisdom? What do the revolutions on the other side of the world have to do with me? And what is the Shift, anyway?

I feel that I am a minute battlefield upon which the ambiguities and wars of this day and age are being fought out.
There is in fact no choice but to humbly put oneself at the disposal of the problems and let oneself be turned into a battleground by them.
For the problems need a refuge.
They must find a place where they can flare up and calm down. We, the poor little people, have to open our inner room for them.
We cannot run away.
—Etty Hillesum, Holocaust victim

What we do have for inspiration are these stories that have been passed on by word of mouth for generations. These stories come from a dreamier time to instruct the soul in the basics of behavior and morality. Myths and fairy tales speak the soul's language. The brilliance of these stories is that there is no One Truth. We bring our experience to any understanding, and understanding to every experience. Pictorial consciousness lends itself to interpretation and discussion in contrast to linear thought, which tends to be only intellectual and adhere to specific content.

The rational mind understands literal translations and thoughts it has already had: "This is a black dog," requires no additional information. Pictorial thinking describes the experiential consciousness of indigenous cultures, and children, and the point at which many women begin to start taking responsibility for their thinking. Pictorial thinking is more difficult to articulate than the linear thought with which the Western world has been built. Pictorial thinking can be fleeting because mercurial images occur simultaneously. Without the harnessing power of a person's sacred individuality, feelings, which are made of pictures, lack direction and personal meaning.

Through the images of mythology, we see how the gods walked among us and how their temperaments explained the unexplainable. They were the science of their day. Fairy tales, on the other hand, have a moral component. Although we generally think of them as intended for young children, these tales inform the child in all of us. Archetypical images interact to educate the soul about the meaning of hardship, trials, and mastery of perceived evil. J.R. Tolkien, George MacDonald, and Rudolf Steiner are a few who have written stories for all ages; these tales challenge the soul and dream life to dig more deeply and to connect a little more strongly to the stories of destiny we live every day.

There are four distinct stages of a fairy tale—fantasy, escape, recovery, and consolation. This may be a universal format, but there is no One Truth. Each person has his or her life experience and relationship with archetypes that illuminate each story in a personal way. Fairy tales, myths, religions, and science, for that matter, offer a banquet of images for the soul's evolution, but only if we have the imagination to understand the message.

Stories are medicine… They have such power; they do not require that we do, be, act anything—we need only listen. The remedies for repair or reclamation of any lost psychic drive are contained in stories.
—Clarissa Pinkola Estes, PhD

My life's work began once I started working with pictorial consciousness and acquainted myself with archetypes. Fairy tales steadied my faint heart and opened doors to the miraculous, to a more imaginative world—a world of magic and elementals. Through these living imaginations, my soul was able to relax and be enveloped by a destiny that put my life into context. In these living imaginations of Life's complexities, it is not the cleverest, smartest, or most beautiful who wins. Adversity comes to us all. My struggles are not punishment for deviating from some imaginary path, but instead are a part of the human struggle to consciousness, and the use of power and control. Nobody escapes the initiation of Selfhood. Power is the active ingredient to the ever-evolving crisis and triumph of everyday evolution. The aspiring must learn to direct authority (or power) or be used by it. The good-hearted, the ones who are kind to nature, do triumph in the end. The rightful princess prevails, and the kingdom is restored. What was once upon a time is now. We have a kingdom to restore.

The ancient myths (and fairy tales) were
designed to harmonize body and soul.
—Joseph Campbell

Our kingdom can be likened to the Grimm's fairy story of *"The Goose Girl."* It is a part of fairy tale literature in France, Germany, and England. In all three places, the story shares the same format, and it is one of my personal favorites. It should come as no surprise that everybody has a Feminine and Masculine aspect to his or her being. If this is so, then the story of the princess is everyone's story. In the world of duality, everything has a shadow. The stepmother is a shadow of the Feminine, as is the maid-in-waiting, or the false princess, in this tale. As a culture, we have given away an important quality of the human psyche to this shadow of the Truth.

In this tale, an old queen sends her beloved daughter to a faraway kingdom to be married to a prince. She sends with her a maid-in-waiting, silver and gold, trinkets, and jewelry as befitting a royal dowry. They each have a horse. The princess's horse, Falada, is magical and can speak. The queen cuts herself with a knife and lets three drops of blood fall on a hanky that the true princess tucks away in her bodice for safekeeping. After they have ridden a while, and when they cross a stream, the princess requests that the maid-in-waiting dismount and fetch her drink. The maid is not only disrespectful, but defiant, and tells the princess that if she wants a drink, to get off of her high horse and get it herself. She says, "I do not choose to be your servant." For the first time, we hear the three drops of blood lament, "If this your mother knew, her heart would break in two."

The story does start in the world of fantasy, in the undifferentiated world of once upon a time. We don't hear about any Masculine influence—king or other father figure—who protects his beloved daughter. We get the sense that this may be the queen's last-ditch effort to save her royal line. The Queen Mother loves her daughter and sends her away with family treasure and a reminder of her royal bloodline in the three drops of blood. The princess begins her journey to autonomy but does not have any power of her own. She cannot think for herself, and lives in a child-like dream, and so does the bidding of her mother and then her maid-in-waiting. When we learn to perceive what is real for ourselves, we learn to think and negotiate Life's tribulations. Real thinking is synthetic in nature and goes beyond the mere facts, figures, and words of someone else's experience. The intellect can pose as real thinking: however, living thought is creative and the only source of individual freedom. Disjointed and random thoughts reflect a person who is ineffective and vulnerable. Without conviction, the princess's words have no power or authority. She expresses a wish and not a resolve. The princess is humbled, says nothing, and mounts her horse again.

The travelers continue on, cross another stream, and the princess once again tells the serving maid to get her a drink. Once again, the serving maid refuses to obey. The true princess dismounts, but this time…floats away. This time when she stoops to drink, the hanky with the three drops of blood falls from her bodice and floats away. As it floats away we hear, "If your mother only knew, it would break her heart in two." The maid-in-waiting sees this happen and knows that without drops of blood, the true princess will forget her heritage and then she, the maid in waiting will have power over the to-be-bride.

Before the princess is able to remount, the serving maid demands they switch places, horses, clothing, and purpose. The princess is compelled to swear by the blue sky above that she would not reveal one word of this to anyone and if she did, she would surely die. With this coup d'état complete, they continue on.

Time and time again, we hear the lament, and what a lament it is! "If your mother only knew, it would break her heart in two." No one may help the princess, not even her mother. As an initiation, she must face her trials by herself. The primal fear of being left all alone is not only a great fear to a child but also strikes deep in the heart of the mature. The young princess has not been adequately prepared for what she meets in the world. Tragically, she forgets that royalty flows in her blood and that she is the true princess.

Every character in the tale is some part of the reader, even the basic motif that we are descendants of a royal bloodline. The princess rides the magical white horse that is a symbol of pure thought, but even so, Falada is taken from her. She hasn't had the life experience to know how to use her thinking. She is incapable of fending for herself and she is by no means a match for the false princess. The shadow element, as the maid-in-waiting, takes over as materialistic false personality or, as Jung would call it, the animus.

The shadow is an overlooked force of the human personality. It drives individuals and runs governments, causing wars and ruining countries and lives. We'll examine this director of destiny later as the shadow is ever- present, underestimated, and potentially dangerous. Here in the physical world, all forms have a shadow; even the illuminating light of a lit candle has a shadow life.

Upon arrival, the true princess is shuffled off to be a goose girl and Falada, her magical horse, is silenced, its head nailed to the town gate. Only the head, or head thinking, remains. She no longer has a magical horse. Every day when the true princess leaves the town to take the geese to pasture, she hears the horse lament, "If your mother only knew, it would break her heart in two."

Conrad helps her tend the geese, although he is most definitely more interested in attending to her. Every day he wants to touch her hair, but she calls to the wind in what sounds like an incantation, "Blow wind, blow I say. Blow Conrad's hat away. Make him chase it here and there until I've tied up all my hair." Conrad spends the rest of the day chasing his hat. He becomes fed up with the drama and goes to the old king with his complaint.

The old king finds the story curious and commands Conrad to drive the flock out the next day. The king hears the true princess speak to the head of Falada, call to the wind, and wonders what sort of maiden commands the elements.

Geese communicate with one another all the time. Never silent, they communicate with themselves and their gaggle. The goose archetype can be understood as this: if you don't communicate with others, no one can help you. The geese tending represents acts of service that must be done every day, like chopping wood and carrying water. Through adversity, the rightful princess evolves and this time when the princess meets opposition, she doesn't acquiesce; she has a plan. Conrad sees her only as a girl, and a girl of little consequence. She uses her creative words to direct the outcome of *this* trial. And, this time, she has learned to say, "NO."

The king, who already sensed something is different about her, now asks her story. She keeps her promise of silence because she has sworn to the heavens above her. But the king tells her to tell her sorrows to the iron stove. The princess demonstrates integrity by keeping her word in the face of all that has gone wrong, but there is no sorrow like a broken heart. She pours out her tale and opens her heart so the king can hear. Here is an important point in the story. The true princess does not feel like a victim or lament her sorrows to the king. Many of us know that telling our woes does little to change the facts. There is so much we can't convey to others in words.

More things are wrought by prayer
than this world dreams of.
—Alfred, Lord Tennyson

Even though this king has no queen, he is insightful. He tells her to tell her story to the iron stove. Iron represents strength, and the stove itself speaks of the power of the will. This stove is the instrument for the transformation of material substances. The stove is the agent of change. Telling her story to the iron stove with the king listening is an image of heart-filled prayer which can shift the princess's story and bring resolution to her peril. Prayer is an act of faith and can allow the best to come to pass. It is where we appeal to go deeper by connecting to the highest creative spirit. It is an art. If the princess lacked belief, nothing could have happened to change her situation. She did not desert herself, and she was able to articulate what had happened. The mystery of prayer is vast and in my personal experience underutilized. Prayer is how to go deeper into the mystery by connecting with a power much greater than our own. At the end of my rope is where I truly find God. Chances are, we don't pray for circumstance to revert to before but pray for revelation. As we learn to pray, we learn the longing of our hearts. We do not complain but learn to invite. Whining is tacky. A shift in circumstance becomes possible. Part of prayer work is developing the vigilance to recognize the answer when it comes. Never forget to say, "Thank You." and remember, the Time Spirit has a sense of humor.

> *Ask and it shall be given to you; seek and ye*
> *shall find; knock, and it shall be opened unto you.*
> *—Matthew 7:7*

At a banquet the king relates the princess's tale to the false princess; he asks her what the punishment should be for such a person. The false princess tells him in some detail that the person should be stripped naked, put into a spike barrel, and rolled through the street until dead. How does it happen that human beings can inflict such misery on others? Certainly, there is no empathy, compassion, or sympathy; pure intellect with imagination squeezed out. At this point, the King orders this to be the sentence of the false princess. The Shift takes place as it should. The male and female are elevated to their rightful purposes, and all is right with the world.

Personal development requires transcendence, as opposed to the achievement of mere worldly success. There is alchemy of spirit when a person is balanced, and living in harmony with a higher purpose. The false princess pronounces her own fate, by her own words. The price of pronouncing judgment on others is high and a *must-learn* if one is to progress along the path to the rightful kingdom. The king carried out her pronouncement, the young king married his true bride, and both of them reigned over their kingdom in peace and happiness.

SHIFTING

Our times are changing… The Shift is coming. Change will take place with or without our help. I tell my fully adult daughter that Life is designed to chase each one of us into the arms of God. The rocky roads, the twist of fate, and the dark nights of the soul can have a higher purpose. The path is filled with ambiguities and paradoxes like Freedom/Obedience and Autonomy/Surrender that only make sense when lived. At my daughter's age, I feared my autonomy. Autonomy is a grown-up word used to indicate the possibility of acting out of one's insight and personal authority. It is a powerful word for personal growth, as it has the possibility of animating connections. I was afraid if I listened to my spiritual revelation I would end up in a cloister bound by vows that I did not understand and to a God that had no idea what being a human being was like. However, there was no cloister for me. I, like the Goose Girl, made my way into adulthood, unprepared and unaware of the forces and powers that shape the world. These forces, these powers are forever at work. We can grow into being responsible for them, or we can be used by them.

Without the decision to act, we are complicit. In order to gain the wisdom to act, I believe we must stop to ask definitive questions. When learning to measure, you must learn to calculate from zero, not begin at one. Zero is essence. Zero is where it is possible to get to the power behind all of the drama. How do we wake from the sleep that allows life to just happen to us in order to get to the point of authority or be authors of Life?

We must have a pure, honest and warm-hearted motivation and on top of that determination, optimism, hope, and the ability not to be discouraged. The whole of humanity depends on this motivation.
—The Dalai Lama

GETTING TO ZERO

So then because thou art lukewarm, and neither
cold nor hot, I will spue thee out of my mouth.
—Revelation 3:16

Everyone strategically abuses power, authority, and control. Yes, everyone. We each think that somehow we will be different, that my version of reality is better, and that I won't fall victim to the great temptations of Life. History is littered with the souls of naïve or reckless do-gooders. But, unless we are willing to get our hands dirty and get to work, we will end up mired in materialism. The various scenarios are not pretty or compatible with Nature. However, we are not powerless. In fact, the greatest message we can learn is the magnitude of the resource of strength in our core. We human beings have made the drama; we can choose to create something else.

Choosing is a function of intelligence, but choice implies intention. What is the anatomy of decision that is the bedrock of intention? What makes the deed more powerful than a whim? The quality of an intention can be illustrated by the temperature of the decision. Intention emerges from an emotional connection to a *desire* and progresses to ever warmer degrees of self- determination. *Desire* does not necessarily have a progress plan with a specific destination. With *hope, desire* can be quickened by optimism and by faith and may progress from a dream to a hankering, and then to a determination fueled by will-power. A lukewarm decision is hope. "Gee, I *hope* I lose ten pounds." *Hope* is the emergence of desire. A *wish* is more tepid, caused by a weak feeling in connection to the *desire*. At this level of commitment, any number of invading thoughts can derail the best of intentions. For instance, I have played some funny games with myself surrounding food! Has anyone else heard the little voice that assures the hopeful that a bite unseen by others has no calories? The mind is a curious playmate.

> *Until one is committed, there is hesitancy, the chance to draw*
> *back, always ineffectiveness. Concerning all acts of initiation-*
> *creation-there is one elementary truth, the ignorance of*
> *which kill countless ideas and splendid plans.*
> *—Goethe*

When you're hot, your choice carries a resolve that ensures a specific result. It is accompanied by a refined emotion that creates a particular feeling. But the specific feeling is what is important. A *resolve* insures an initiative will take place, no question; it is the initiating virtue necessary to catalyze an intention. Techniques that anticipate change before anger sets in create a self-initiated morality that governs the desired results. The art of action is really a technology of result. A *resolve* follows us into sleep and across the final threshold. Where do we practice *resolve*? Apathy is a precursor to failure. How we order our thoughts, relationships, and household are determined by the intentions and decisions we make. This is where we learn to say *yes* and practice when to say *no*. I lose weight by what I put on my plate and what I put in my mouth. Now this is freedom. The depth of a decision is tested by what we really believe. Marriage is a resolve—at least it should be.

> *Resolve to create a good future.*
> *It's where you'll spend the rest of your life.*
> *—Charles Franklin Kettering*

After I quit smoking, I was approached in a dream with an offer to smoke a cigarette. The moment was lucid, and I was so sure that I did not want to smoke that the temptation was easily overcome. I was awake to my resolve in my dream. These conversations with the voice within are the basis of morality. Morality establishes a sphere of limitation that can change mere synchronicity into conscious coincidence. Consciousness and morality form the chalice of our being. There is a formative force in morality. If thoughts are created by thinking, deeds by intentions and the will, the heart is created by morality. If so, morality is a formative force that can be created by acts based on love.

> *To be really great in little things, to be truly noble and heroic in the insipid*
> *details of everyday life, is a virtue so rare as to be worthy of canonization.*
> *—Harriet Beecher Stowe*

My daughter, like all babies, played at reaching for a ring toy hanging from her crib. A wave of forgetfulness washed over her concentration so many times, but the moment came when her fingers clutched the ring. She held on tight, and the look of triumph on her face was indescribable. Her resolve to capture the ring was undeniable. Children have a mighty resolve to learn to walk. Learning to walk occupies most of their waking moments. They fall down and get up again and again. When or where else can you witness such focus? The child looks to her caretakers for loving guidance and a hand until the final victory is won. In each child's triumph, the human spirit is celebrated anew. Who would want to weaken the child's resolve to grow into all that can be imagined? Our dreams for the future cannot be just hope. Choice for a future we want happens again and again, until it becomes realized by resolve.

Independence, autonomy, individuality, and the ability to determine our future are relatively new concepts in the evolutionary story of human beings, and they are what make the *Shift* possible. We are mesmerized by a paternal culture that values pragmatism, intellect, and cold hard truths. *Beware*—there is a danger of becoming what we react to.

What I have found is that even if you are born into a woman's body, it doesn't mean you don't think and act like a man. What are the qualities that need saving? Traditionally, success has been directly linked, for the most part, to the use and abuse of power. Too often we become what we resist because we fear the great unknown, the dark, and the ocean's depth. We don't venture very far from the shore, or veer too far off the path—for heaven's sake, look what happened to Little Red Riding Hood! Life is calling to each of us and implores that we follow our hearts to make new paths, forged with moral fortitude, by finding the hidden power in our thoughts that are formed out of love and compassion. We must make all things new. The survival of all things precious depends on whether we find the courage to alter what appears to be a rush to oblivion.

Fairy stories are here to tell us that so much is happening below the threshold of our awareness and that our backs are covered by even the timeliness of the event. It is the eleventh hour, almost past time for men and women alike, to wake up to the sleeping Feminine strength inside of us. Revelation and revolutions can happen in the twinkling of an eye.

Only the heart knows how to find what is precious.
—Fyodor Dostoyevsky

FROM YESTERDAY TO TODAY

History has not been kind to women and often depicts them as unworthy collaborators in the real world. Women have been objects to be owned, forced into submission, and demeaned in sport and song. Women have fought for the right to own property and the right to vote. The history of women's suffrage in the United States landed these valiant women in prisons. They were shunned by their husband and families, and, worse yet, committed to insane asylums. This was 1920, only ninety years ago in what is considered a progressive country. Rape, sex trafficking, and marginalization of the weak still make headlines in every town and city in the United States.

According to a National Organization for Women study, one in four women will be sexually assaulted in the course of their college career; the statistics are not entirely accurate as nine out of ten rapes go unreported. An accused rapist is more likely to be acquitted than a person charged with other violent crimes. Furthermore, the perpetrator is likely to be an acquaintance! If this isn't alarming enough, the study exposes that many women just do not know how to say, "No!" or are afraid of hurting someone's feelings. If this isn't alarming enough, the 2012 winner at the Sundance film festival, *"The Invisible War"*, exposed that one in five women have been raped in the course of their military service. The statistics are nothing short of terrifying.

Around the world, women are held hostage by outdated religions and patriarchal societies that deem it socially permissible to maim, torture, burn, and beat wives, daughters, and mothers into submission. There is no sanity to these attacks. Does this attitude speak to latent misogyny in the human psyche or are these behaviors vestiges of an arrested cultural development? Why does a study of history expose these gross abuses of those made weak and marginalized? These abuses become apparent around racial lines, but closer examination reveals an obsession of the strong to devour the innocent and the weak. If this is so, we *must* do something about it. During the Middle Ages, the convent was a legitimate alternative to the material world for women. Life was difficult, there were few refugees, and life was safer behind the veil. Even today, this world is not for the faint-hearted.

The work of women goes largely unnoticed. Housework is hardly regarded as an art, although its mastery creates a measurable difference in the quality of life of the family. It is the patient revelation that comes with housework that informs the soul that Life is about the persistent maintenance that creates a sacred place for the spirit to reside. Moral activity, day after day, creates a body, family, and community that are the basis of the celebration of Life. A successful life is an accumulation of celebrations that forge meaningful connections that make life viable for all. Women are caretakers of this sacred duty.

There is a lot of talk about the Feminine, the Goddess in the Western world as if we as a culture have arrived at some enlightened state regarding the Goddess as soul. One need only look to Hollywood to see what Americans *really* think of the Feminine. What drives the box office today no longer offers the cathartic experience that leaves us feeling as if we have been touched by something deeply human. The superhero, werewolf, and vampire are the new heroes that relate to the hip young man overpowering the innocent. The hero or heroine is no longer human but cartooned, long on violence and short on conversation. Hollywood is creating new stories that drive our collective consciousness and train our young to be warriors.

What are the storylines that create a tomorrow that doesn't feed the collective nightmare? It is time to dig deeply into our life experiences to find the archetypes and a new mythology working to transform a psyche lost in a materialistic, polarized world. We are in great peril if we contemplate remaining as we are now.

CHAPTER 2

Mermaids, the Grail, and Pollywog Tails

"Teach me to hear Mermaids singing ..."
—*John Donne*

On the way to where I'm going, I bumped into the beautiful, seductive, creative, and dynamic mermaid. At first I believed the fish-tailed marvel to be a superficial notion, entertained only by whimsical fantasy. I did not expect to find vibrant archetypes of Feminine dilemmas living close to the surface of waking consciousness. Nor did I expect to find the mermaid who has as many faces as ancient Greece had goddesses. She is no diva or damsel in distress; she is not a princess slumbering in a castle. She is a mythological being that emerged half human, half creature of the sea. The mermaid I encountered has the siren song that has drawn me deeper into the waters of my own subconscious to understand the implications of character and destiny. Her story contains missing pieces to a fragmented world history, broken by cold hard facts, war, and the neglect of a population most in need of Feminine nurturing care. All of her stories are my story as well. She is a guardian of the waters; her domain is sacred wells, springs, rivers, and oceans. She remains connected to the sea, but longs to emerge into the full, waking consciousness of humanity. Her story is the Feminine journey to consciousness.

Tales of merfolk have accompanied and guided the human race since great ice sheets covered the land. The weather was foul and food was scarce. When the days were bleakest, a merman appeared out of a breathing hole in the ice. He sang the first sea chantey and assured the people that if they left everything they knew, he promised warmer days and sandy beaches. Long story short, he directed the tribe south to what we know as Baja, California, where he guided early populations in the basics of living.

The Dogon tribe, who live on the central plateau of Mali south of Niger, believe they were visited by an extraterrestrial race that played an important role in their earthly evolution. They describe these beings as descending from the greater being called Nommo to take the physical form of a dolphin, merman, or mermaid. Nommo was an amphibious being also known as Master of the Waters, who divided his body for the people to feed and drink his body. This race, according to the Dogon, shared advanced astronomical knowledge about Saturn's rings, the moons of Jupiter, and the binary nature of Sirius, the Dog Star.

In Babylonia, Oannes was a fish-tail merman who brought civilization to the people. He taught mankind how to write, sow seeds, and build temples and towers. According to legend, he brought math, geometry, and the arts. By day he instructed the fledging race, but when the sun set, he returned to the sea. These legends remember the merfolk as benevolent creatures with a utopian vision of peace and harmony. Oannes was said to have married Damkina—Queen of Waters—who we could construe was a mermaid herself. She was the sister/wife to Oannes who was also called Nina.

Ancient Hindu cosmology encompasses one whole living force expressed as *Trimurti*; as having three forms: Brahma, the Creator, Shiva, the Destroyer, and Vishnu, the Preserver. Vishnu is the most renowned of the three. He has repeatedly incarnated into the evolution of the Earth in times of crisis to counteract evil and to preserve and protect the world. As Matysa, Vishnu's first incarnation, appeared to Manu, the first and pious man of the human race. As Manu washed his hands in a river, a little fish pleaded with him to save his life. Manu put it in a jar, but it grew so quickly that Manu had to find larger vessels to contain the fish. Finally, he had to release the fish into the ocean. What had appeared as a small fish grew in significance until the fish revealed itself as Vishnu, a man with a fishtail. Vishnu warned Manu that within seven days a deluge would destroy all life. The fish/ man commanded Manu to take all medicinal herbs, all varieties of seeds, other animals, seven saints, and the serpent Vasuki onto a boat which was then pulled out to sea by a gigantic golden fish. Vishnu, the fish-tailed merman, saved the human race from destruction. His other incarnations have been progressively more refined to include Krishna and Buddha. Vishnu's consort is the lovely Lakshmi, the goddess of auspiciousness and prosperity.

> *Oh, grant me my prayer that I may never lose the*
> *touch of the One in the play of the many.*
> *Rabindranath Tagore*

There are many fish-tailed goddesses with temples throughout the Mediterranean regions dedicated to her as the Mother of Life, or depicted as the Great Mother. As Atagartis, she is depicted as a mermaid, and lavishly festooned with jewels. She was the lady goddess of the sea and responsible for the protection and well-being of those she served. Atagartis's story became entwined with other cultures.

The Greek goddess of love and beauty, Aphrodite, can also be linked to Atagartis. Aphrodite was not begotten in any human sense. Cronus cut off Uranus' genitals and threw them into the sea. This was Aphrodite's beginning! She emerged on the sea foam fully formed and lovely to stand on her own two feet. She is the goddess who connects sea and land. In the Roman pantheon she is Venus, and remembered as the evening star. Though the sea goddesses become a jumble of deities, remnants of her presence remain in Feminine mythologies that can be traced back to the original creation myths, including Adam and Eve and their fall from the Garden of Eden.

Since this time, mermaid lore has appeared all over the world including, but not limited to, such diverse places as India, Switzerland, Norway, Scotland, Thailand, Nigeria, and New Zealand. While seemingly mythological, mermaids remain alive and well in our collective imagination.

While teaching in a small high school here in Missouri, a young girl, seemingly out of nowhere, blurted out, "I want to be a mermaid. I want to grow my hair long and move to California where I can be a mermaid in Disneyland!" And then, while waiting for a plane in St. Louis, I saw two little girls (one age six, and one age eight) busily drawing mermaids. I asked their mother if they had recently seen Johnny Depp's new movie costarring these mavens of the deep. She told me that mermaids had been companions of her daughters since they could draw. The mermaid is alive and well, even here in Missouri. It is no wonder the mermaid excites visions of Feminine strength and playful delight in the minds of her believers; she is autonomous, yet a part of the mysterious ocean. She is pure Nature.

THE SELKIE

Merfolk are not the only feminine psychologies defined by fin or scales. There have been Selkie sightings from Sweden to Canada, and all along the Irish and Scottish coasts. A Selkie is most often described as a woman, strong and stately, wrapped in a seal's skin. Seals slip effortlessly through the waves as if moving to some music of their own. While camping in the Montana de Oro State Park and investigating a tidal pool, I had the distinct impression that someone, not something, was observing my every movement. Turning, I locked eyes with a seal. I saw her watching me and wondered what she had seen. Her eyes were so disarmingly human that I felt a kinship flash between us. Splash and she was gone.

A Selkie feels bone white and ugly without her skin.
—Amanda Adams

It is easy to believe the story of Selkies that appear most notably off the coast of Scotland and the Orkney Islands. Here the gray seal lives, the fog hugs the shore, and seagulls soar, mournfully calling across the waters. Selkies are shape-shifters, some say, formed supernaturally from drowned souls. Legend has it that on the twelfth Holy Night, January 6, Selkies swim into caves and onto beaches where they shed their skin to enjoy a night of dancing and songs. If a young man has a mind to capture one for a wife, he must wait for her to disrobe, seize the opportunity, and steal her seal skin. Even though she may shriek in such a way that a stone would show pity, he must take courage. Selkies are known to make wonderful, dutiful wives. That is, as long as you keep her seal skin safely hidden. Her home and family are her primary focus, but she always has an eye for the sea. She is resigned to her fate as long as there is no chance of recovering her skin. Her community may consider her aloof, for she is a loner whose ambivalent demeanor betrays a depth of soul few understand. The Selkie loses her skin and comes under the control of her captor. She becomes powerless. If given the opportunity to find her seal skin, she quickly abandons her captor, home, and children to return to the sea. Her story is that of every one of us who has ever avoided capture, or feared the lock in wedlock. Few blushing brides today include "obey" in their vows and many of us resist changing our maiden name to disappear into the ranks of Mrs. There is strength in a chosen name; it can have the protective quality of the seal's skin. A name can have a resonance that functions as an anointing or mantle when it is given at birth or initiation. Protected, the sacred individuality can mature to stand on solid ground.

THE LITTLE MERMAID

The Little Mermaid is an original tale written in 1837 by Hans Christian Anderson. He wove aspects of mythology, his understanding of human nature, and the work of Paracelsus, a Swiss alchemist/scholar, to fuse a story that has enjoyed timeless popularity. Since then, it has been danced on the stage, sung before audiences all over the world, and celebrated in paintings and sculptures. Disney took Hans Christian Anderson's story of the Little Mermaid, but obscured the story enough that all that is left is a sentimental tale of a young mermaid longing for yet another prince. Disney doesn't tell us how she longed for a human soul, or that she willingly, though hesitantly, allowed her tongue to be cut from her mouth just to get a crack at being human. Tragically, the Little Mermaid yearns to be someone she is not. When she reaches her fifteenth birthday, her grandmother tells her that she is now old enough to venture to the surface of the sea to find out about the world of men. There she falls in love with a prince. She approaches the sea witch or "serving maid," as was the case in the Goose Girl tale, and arranges to cash in her beautiful voice for a pair of legs. The sea witch gives her a poisonous drink that cuts through her body like a double-edged sword (many of our decisions have a double edge) to transform her tail into a pair of legs. In the transformation, she suffers pain as if knives were piercing her feet with every step (sounds like stilettos to me!). Never mind the pain! What was important was *that she was more beautiful and graceful than ever!* When she relinquishes her beautiful voice, she also loses the ability to tell her personal story. In the end, she doesn't wed the prince or live happily ever after. When she fails to marry the prince, she is told that her heart will break and that she will not be allowed to be human or a mermaid ever again. She is banished from all she has known and must join the spirits of the air. There she will earn her human soul after three hundred years of selfless service to others.

Becoming real or human can be torturous, and the initiations heart-wrenching. The heart of the story is the heart; the story's greatest lesson to be learned is to be loved and to love in return. Hans Christian Anderson's story reveals the secret aspirations of all creation to be loved. Not only the Little Mermaid, but the waves of the ocean and the air we breathe look forward to having consciousness bestowed upon them. The art of Nature is in the human heart. But this story has been so "revised" that the grim repercussions for her untimely desire go unnoticed.

One must suffer to be beautiful.
—The Little Mermaid's grandmother

Women have gone to great lengths to become what they are not—waist cinches, bustles, spike heels, botox, breast reduction, breast augmentation, cellulite suction, tummy tucks, face lifts, eye lifts, nose surgery, hair color, braces; and then there are the antidepressants that keep the soul from collapsing from the loss of her personal story. The photo-shopped model is now the latest assault on self-esteem for all of us who never did measure up to the cultural image of beauty. Even in this enlightened society that we fancy we are living in, the woman who feels at home in her body is the exception to the rule.

What makes a woman beautiful? Many of my women friends who are aging along with me are struggling with this question. Some of us have arrived at our maturity with a false sense of worth, cultivated by looks that could open doors and get a free drink on Friday nights. There is a lot of collateral in being young and beautiful. These women are finding it either very expensive or deeply transformative to grapple with the Western

Cult of Beauty and Personality that tries to dictate a person's self- worth and relevance. If one is too mesmerized by one's own reflection, beauty can be a difficult taskmaster. A soul can feel empty, cut-off from the experience of an authentic voice. How a woman comes to terms with her body is the deciding point of her happiness. The looking glass that a mermaid is sometimes known to possess may have once been for verification of personal beauty, but now it can be used for self-reflection.

MELUSINE OF THE FOURTEENTH CENTURY

"The story of Melusine came to signify for me the difficulty that women have living in a man's world—almost as if women belong to another element."
—Phillippa Gregory The White Queen

These words belong to Phillippa Gregory who incorporated the story of the mermaid Melusine into her novel, *The White Queen*. It is an historical novel that follows Elizabeth Woodville's rise to royalty. What made her ascent notable was that Elizabeth was the first commoner to marry an English sovereign, and she considered herself a blood relative to Melusine. There is some evidence she may have called upon the pre-Christian mermaid to secure her position in court. She was tried for witchcraft, but never convicted. Elizabeth was the last queen of the Plantagenet house who was defeated in the War of the Roses (1437–1992) by the Christian House of Tudor. Her story marks the demise of the pagan mysteries and the rise of Christianity. Her story connects, through Elizabeth, Richard I (who some call Arthur, the Rose of England) to Avalon, and makes Elizabeth the maternal grandmother of Henry VIII.

So who is this mermaid who meddles in history and whose blood flows through nobility? Folk wisdom places her throughout the north Celtic regions of France, Poland, and throughout Christendom. In Germany, she appeared as a heraldic figure and was depicted with a crown and two scaly tails, one draped over each arm. Some areas also gave her wings. In 1807, Goethe wrote a tale about her titled, *"Die Neue Melsuina."* Most notably, perhaps, you have seen her gracing a cup of your morning coffee from Starbucks. A modern-day women's magazine has been named after her and I have read some speculation that Melusine was the CIA code name for Hillary Clinton!

To know her better, we should begin with her beginnings, with her mother, the fay or fairy Pressina. The story originated in a forest in Albania (some say Luxembourg) where King Elinas followed a beautiful song to find the fay Pressina. He fell in love with her beauty and her magic and proposed marriage. She accepted, on the condition she be allowed solitude at the time of her lying in, or childbirth.

In due time, Pressina gave birth to three daughters: Melusine or Melusina (as she is also called), Melior, and Palatina. The king, in his enthusiasm, rushed to see his wife, forgetting his promise. He barged in on her as she was bathing the babies. He knew there was nothing he could do now. He promised more than he could deliver, and he broke his word. Much to his dismay, Pressina left in a whirl and took the girls from the castle to live on the secluded magical island of Avalon.

The girls were raised under the best of circumstances, but were always reminded why they had to leave the castle and the pleasures of the court. Melusine grew bitter, and on her fifteenth birthday she conjured a plan to punish her father. Together, the sisters cast a spell to steal their father's fortune and then lock him in a high mountain.

When Pressina discovered their plot, she became enraged with her daughters and punished each of them in accordance with their responsibility. Melusine, the eldest and the most responsible, was cursed to become a mermaid once a week—some accounts declare Wednesdays, others say Saturdays. She was cast out of Avalon. Melusine wandered to modern-day France, Northern Gaul, where, in the forest, she met Raymondin. He was involved in a hunting accident and witnessed a wild pig murder his uncle.

Melusine comforted him by telling him that he was faultless and that he should return to his castle as if nothing had happened.

He so appreciated her counsel and her beauty that he fell in love with her and begged her to marry him.

Now mind you, Raymondin was the first guy to come along, but Melusine seriously considered the proposal. Her term of the union was that she be allowed sanctuary every Saturday and that her privacy never be disturbed on this day. Some legends say Raymondin built her a castle for her Saturday rendezvous; others say that on her wedding night she magically conjured up her castle. Either way, the castle was a formidable one, but there was a fatal flaw in the story.

Melusine never confided her true nature to her husband. She gave birth to sons, but the boys were both beastly and deformed. Raymondin so loved Melusine that his heart was not compromised. On the surface, the couple appeared to be happy and she was allowed to continue her privacy every Saturday.

Raymondin never questioned her motives until one night, when a hunter knocked at the door to ask for shelter. In the course of the conversation, Raymondin told the hunter about Melusine's weekly departures. By questioning Melusine's motives, the hunter planted seeds of distrust in Raymondin's heart. The thought of his wife having a clandestine meeting plagued him until, in spite of his promise, he had to know where she went each week. He plotted to expose her motives. Different renditions have different consequences for his breach of trust. In one tale, she grew wings to fly away; in another, her bath was swallowed up by the earth; and in yet another, she immediately left with a broken heart, betrayed and bemoaning that *her greatest secret had been stolen.*

Many women have a secret that must be nurtured in times of artful solitude. We need a time and place where we can be alone and know we are loved. Although I have never grown a tail in my bathtub, I am critically aware that my soul life is tidal and that I, like Melusine, need time to dream, conjure my future, transform energy, and listen to the slight whispers that can otherwise go unnoticed in a busy world. This time of reflection has proven vital to the process of my continually emerging Self. Perhaps, if her beloved had understood the need for a sacred space, he could have been spared her disappearance. How could Melusine have foreseen a recapitulation of her mother's destiny? Once again, a promise was broken and the Feminine was misunderstood or not taken seriously.

You must have a room or certain hour of the day or so where you can simply experience and bring forth what you are and what you might be…At first you may find nothings happening—but if you have a sacred place and use it, take advantage of it, something will happen.
—*Joseph Campbell*

Melusine sightings are still spoken about when the wind howls and breezes sigh. In Czechoslovakia and Slovenia, the word for these wailing winds is *meluzine.* She is the white lady who haunts the forest and tricks mortals with riddles, or dances in the garden to foretell of a death in the house. She has even been legitimized as Saint Melusine in Germany, where on Christmas Eve some families shake breadcrumbs on the ground for her.

RUSALKI OF RUSSIA

The Rusalki is a Slavic rebel, cowgirl, and mermaid who leads a raucous life, and defies tradition in order to live a life free of responsibility and societal expectations. These remarkable creatures bask in the adoration of their suitors and readily accept their gifts. The Slavic Rusalki is believed to be the reincarnated spirit of the young and jilted who died before their time, un- baptized and with a broken heart. She is strikingly beautiful, the color of a moody sea, with long unkempt hair that is unbound and therefore forever in a tangle. The Rusalki loves a good party. The modern-day ones I know have names like Marcy, Penny, and Mary Catherine, and drink margaritas or beer.

Well-behaved women seldom make history.
—Lauren Thatcher, Ulrich

In the Russian countryside, the Rusalki homeland, the customs and expectations for young girls are still specific. How she wears her hair reflects her age and marital status. While young and single, she may embellish a long single braid, but upon marriage she is required to wear two braids wrapped and hidden beneath a head covering. The Rusalki, of course, defies tradition and lets her beautiful locks flow freely about her body.

Women who seek to be equal with men lack ambition.
—Timothy Leary

When a marriage match is made for a girl, (arranged marriage is alive and well in this twenty-first century. Three-fourths of the marriages in India are still arranged) the men—future groom, the girl's father, and the matchmaker— pray together, light candles, and drink wine while the girl's hair is ceremoniously covered with a kerchief. She sits alone with that swatch of linen on her head, a light hand of new ownership upon her scalp. Amid the deep-voiced mumblings and frequent handshakes, the bride-to-be overhears the trajectory of her life discussed and mapped without her ...

As her wedding day draws near, her hair is repeatedly lathered with honey and butter. Her girlfriends, even her brothers, wash and comb the girl's hair until it is lustrous and moisturized, sleek with sweet saturation. They braid it and then wash it, braid it and then wash it once more. And if anyone squeezes the bride's locks with both hands, honey pours out. This cycle of grooming the bride's hair lasts several days. While the day of the wedding arrives, the bride's girlfriends drink her bathwater in the hope that they too may be so fortunate as to find husbands.

En route to the ceremony, the bride's hair, for the first and last time in her public life, is let loose…The bride's disheveled hair is deliberately allowed to hang wild and free only so that it may (be) captured and restrained…In the relinquishing of her unbound locks, the bride hands over her freedom and autonomy, for life.

—A Mermaid's Tale, page 171

The notion that a woman's hair should be covered and her beauty veiled is by no means isolated to the Russian countryside. Here in Missouri, an Amish woman wears a cap to conceal her uncut hair, which the Amish believe is a woman's crowning glory. Across the world, in the Middle East, the Taliban's patriarchal regime maintains a rigorous public presence. Sharia law dictates a woman's public and private life. Here, a young girl's hair may go uncovered. However, a pubescent girl must cover herself from head to toe with the woman's uniform, the burka, whenever she leaves the safety of her home. The burka is an enveloping outer garment that is designed to make women literally invisible. Hidden behind the veil, she poses no threat to the patriarchal society nor is the weak man seduced by his sexual fantasies. Women live in public obscurity to save men from themselves.

The making of invisibility is by no means the only harsh treatment in patriarchal societies that young women are forced to endure. In Northeast Africa, and parts of the Near East and Southeast Asia, girls are unceremoniously coerced to suffer female genital mutilation. According to the World Health Organization, the procedures involve partial or total removal of the external female genitalia. Amnesty International estimates this procedure is inflicted on two million girls every year.

In the extreme, the procedure narrows the vagina by the creation of a covering flap of skin to make a seal. The wound is held together to heal with a thorn or stitching. In some cases, the girl's legs must be tied together for two to six weeks to allow healing to take place. All that remains of an opening is to allow urine to pass and menstrual blood to flow. The procedure can be performed in a hospital setting, but it often takes place in the bush where it is done by an older woman or even the child's own mother

The World Health Organization, as well as other human rights organizations, has campaigned to eliminate this practice, but they have found it difficult to influence such deep-seated cultural behaviors. Many communities do not question the legitimacy of the practice or have long forgotten the reason for performing it altogether. The procedure is thought to guarantee virginity at the time of marriage, so without the scars, a woman has no proof of virtue and can be considered a social outcast.

SEE TO BE

In some cases, the experiences of different marginalized groups can present unique challenges. The story of the mermaid is still synonymous in the subconscious with the tangle of men struggling with passionate desires and all that is not holy in the soul. She is no longer the voice of the harmony of the spheres but lures the righteous (man) to a watery grave. She is a warning of the deadly consequences of lust. The mermaid has become a caricature of the Feminine. While progress has been made, women continue to face distinct obstacles in the pursuit of equality. If the Feminine qualities of compassion, unconditional love, nurturing, care for the land, care for children, art, and celebration are not included or honored, society as a whole is crippled. Men have a Feminine component to their soul-life that is in jeopardy as well, and it is not being hunted by the treacherous woman, but often held captive because it does not yet have a voice. Media dictates social standards for both girls and boys, perpetuating narrow ideals of beauty and masculinity. We need more diverse and balanced representations of women and men.

Understanding discrimination only as racial is only part of the unholy dilemma. Discrimination takes place because of a hunger or lust in the human soul for power and control. This pathology stems from an animalistic passion to devour the weak and control the innocent. This is not an abstraction; this is a tendency that is clearly expressed today in world politics, capitalism, and the subjugation of Nature. Everybody wants Power, and everyone wants to be on top; it is not just the White, Anglo-Saxon Protestant (man) who has fallen victim to this distorted thinking. What passes for thinking in most discourse may be clear, but it is linear and materialistic; it is not real thinking.

It is a product of the intellect that bases its claim to authority on what has been. The past is easy enough to prove with quantifiable statistics. However, with only the rational mind at work, where is the possibility of what might be? There is an indefinable presence that has been lost in the dark waters of the subconscious. An enlightened education is the shortest distance between the mind and the dormant powers of the will. Imagination is the key to insight and solving problems made by the lack of it. Individual genius is necessary to derive meaning from symbolic content or to decode the following:

R/E/A/D/I/N/G   DEATH-LIFE   ECNALG   <u>MIND</u> MATTER

These solutions do not magically fall from heaven, but rise from the depths the mermaid calls home. In the name of science and rationality, this intellectual force masquerades as intelligence, when, in effect, it is empty and lacks imagination. The intellect may be considered a type of thinking, but with the imagination squeezed out.

Women must be the pioneers in this turning inward for strength. In a sense, she has always been the pioneer.
—Anne Morrow Lindbergh

Fairy tales, gnomes, and mermaids remind us that imagination is fostered by going into the dark waters or entering the forest of transformation. Facing the unknown is the key to insight. Without imagination, it is impossible to love because what is essential is invisible to the eye. Without imagination, the ideal, the archetype, is excluded. One need not believe in mermaids to respect the qualities attributed to the invisible powers of the subconscious.

ANSWERS:

READING BETWEEN THE LINES   **LIFE AFTER DEATH**

BACKWARDS GLANCE   **MIND OVER MATTER**

The mermaid was an integral part of the medieval land and seascape up until the twelfth century. She was a peaceful and benevolent creature whose laughter could be heard in the splashing waters of sacred wells, and whose presence explained many of the forces of Nature. The mermaid was included with other furious creatures to indicate uncharted waters where danger and dragons could be encountered. Whether she was a figment of imagination or flesh and blood, her presence as an archetype was real; she was half-sea of dreams and half-mortal flesh.

The day before, when the Admiral was going to the
Rio del Oro, he said he saw three mermaids
who came quite high out of the water
but were not as pretty as they are depicted for
somehow in the face they look like men. He said that he
saw some in Guinea on the coast of Maneguetta.
From the Diary of Christopher Columbus January 9, 1493

Her image was then adapted by the medieval church to symbolize the temptations that men, mostly, had to overcome to achieve salvation and immorality. The mermaid came to symbolize the wanton woman who could cast a spell upon the unsuspecting. Mermaids were real enough that the church banned them from prayer and prohibited them from attending mass. The mermaid was silenced, and monks and priests patrolled the invisible realm of their parishioner's psyches. Angels may have occupied the heavens, but on earth, the mermaid was banned from the altar. The status of women fared no better. History, written by men, has overlooked and undervalued the contributions and challenges women have faced. The choice between harlot and saint has long been a confusing conundrum for many of us.

The human race as a whole is struggling to consciousness, as we face even our own modern-day superstitions. We cannot possibly know what it is to be a human being until the split between the Masculine and the Feminine is radically redefined. The relationship of the two creates a new One. This psychic split is a microcosmos of an equally dangerous split. Our beloved planet is writhing under the burden of our lack of awareness of the bonds that connect us to Nature, body, and soul. Alienated from our earthly mother, we endanger all human life. Corporations may have the legal status as people, but land and resources have no legal standing; nature is property. In the words of Mari Margo at the *2009 Bioneers Convention*, "Who will speak for the trees?" Why can Nestle mine fresh water in the United States to sell overseas or how can old-growth redwoods be endangered by logging companies? How do we say, "No!" to the engineering of the weather? Who will stand up for the rights of animals? On the surface of daily discourse, everything looks like business as usual, but these are desperate times!

Even though there are many feminine archetypes, Western culture is still polarized in its ability to distinguish the subtle nuances that are the life-giving qualities that can be attributed to the Feminine. There are good reasons women have been caretakers, teachers, secretaries, and nurses. I worked two summers in the seed lettuce fields in the Coachella Valley in California. The seed company hired women because women are able to do work that requires attention to detail and we are, or at least were, willing to settle for less money and prestige. Women know that the process determines the product; they pay attention to detail and can do the invisible work behind the scenes. This is a good part of why they are invisible! Who enjoys work that, once completed, must be completed again the same way, the very next day? But, here in the invisible, women develop the confidence in the invisible forces to persevere in the face of an apparent lack of reward. This is, in fact, a definition of faith. Women have kept the faith.

DID GOD HAVE A WIFE?

Antiquity informs us that He did. It took no time at all after his death. Events in the desert did not bring the people to their knees. They gave up their precious metals to craft the Golden Calf. Ancient Hindu religion venerated Durga, and Egypt had Isis. Greece honored Hera who made it into the Roman pantheon as Juno. In the Nordic tradition, Frigg was the Mother Goddess of Creation. Zarathustra abstracted gender to cast Light and Dark as the forces of creation; the resulting drama was about the same. These myths express the oftentimes raucous relationship between the principles of Masculine and Feminine. In polytheistic accounts of creation, both masculine sun god and earth mother or sea goddess had an equal hand in Creation.

There was a brief time in Egyptian antiquity when Akhenaton, the tenth Pharaoh of the 18th dynasty, tried to bring about a departure from traditional polytheist worship. Aten, the One God, was represented as the magnificent disc of the sun and Akhenaton was the Sun's miraculously begotten son. The surviving murals of this time depart from a stylized depiction of the pharaoh to show him not at all idealized, but as he really appeared: a family man with his son upon the knee of his beautiful wife, Nefertiti. Another mural shows the Sun's rays animated with hands to bestow blessings upon the happy couple. Akhenaton was a prophet before his time but was considered a heretic after his passing. His people never truly gave up their beloved idols. It took but ten years after his death for a reformation to obscure evidence that the Egyptians ever entertained a solitary deity. The archaeological record of his reign reveals statues and murals were either defaced or destroyed in an attempt to discredit his influence. The belief in One God did not emerge again for another two hundred years when Moses went to the mountaintop for his revelation of the One God. Even then, his people were not ready to give up the Golden Calf.

Moses destroyed the tablets of the Ten Commandments in an angry rage precisely because the people had such a visceral connection to the many gods and goddesses of their past. Within the Ten Commandments was the codification of moral behavior that would galvanize Judah into the Jewish people we know today. The leap from polytheistic deities to a monotheistic Father God was not an overnight success, but slowly took place in the course of Hebrew history.

No Gentile can dispute the sorrows our Jewish brothers and sisters have endured in forging what many consider the founding story of Western Culture. The tribes of Judah were the chosen people to live this struggle as a demonstration of the cathartic evolution of consciousness. They forgot, they fell, and were forgiven so many times as a testament to God's love and forgiveness of Creation's children. Here is the evolution of our human understanding of God which is, in fact, the evolution of the human race.

It is difficult to imagine what society must have been like in this tribal community. Their consciousness would bear no resemblance to our fast-paced secular culture. They were hardly monotheist but emerged from Canaanite pagan roots. If we could return to the eighth century BC, we would find these tribes worshiping not only Baal but also his Feminine counterpart. *The Hebrew Bible* mentions this Queen of Heaven no less than forty times, even calling her the consort of Yahweh. *The Old Testament* describes her as the goddess par excellence whose name revealed someone mighty and nurturing. *The Book of Kings* describes how female attendants in the temple wove ritual textiles for her and also how to prepare little cakes for her festival. Her name was Asherah; translated as – *she who subdues the sea.* There is considerable evidence that Asherah was worshipped right alongside Yahweh in the temple in Jerusalem.

In 1967 Raphael Patoi was the first historian to mention that the Hebrew Yahweh had a Feminine counterpart. His theory was further justified by artifacts found in the Sinai desert in 1975. Archeologists uncovered an eighth-century shard of pottery with an inscription that can be translated with the following inscription, *"I have blessed you by* YHVH *by Yahweh and by his Asherah."* Since then, more amulets, ancient texts, and figures have been uncovered. The BBC aired a three-part documentary - *DID GOD HAVE A WIFE?* - based on the journals, books, and lectures of Francesca Stavrakopoulou.

Times were hard and war was common, resulting in slavery and exile to foreign lands for the losers. Historically, the Israelites found themselves in captivity time and time again. In 586 BC, the elite community within Judea was exiled to Babylon; the Temple in Jerusalem was burned. History tells us of the anguish the people experienced in captivity and the drastic reforms the priesthood pursued in order to regain God's favor. In II Kings 23, Josiah recommitted himself to the covenant with God; he burned idols and scattered ashes upon the graves of the children. *Hear, O Israel, the Lord our God, our God our Lord, is One Lord. (Deuteronomy 6;4)*

This is my conjecture: Here is the story of how the human race emerged from the shadowy life of superstition and idolatry. The population was guided by a priesthood that totally relied on vision and revelation to understand the complexities of God's intentions. They, I am sure, did not possess the methodical powers of discernment that have slowly awakened in human thought. And, might I add, they were all men. The rabbinical conversation examined why they found themselves enslaved in Babylon, Samaria, and by the Philistines. The revelation of a solitary God came with a warning that if they continued to offer sacrifices to the pagan gods and goddesses He, the Almighty, would send nations to enslave and punish them. Yes, there was and is One God. There is One creative force at work throughout Creation. There is One unified field of consciousness. Extreme reforms needed to be accomplished for humanity to evolve out of superstition. Belief in a One God who encompassed all of Creation was central to the evolution of an individual capable of a creative focus. This creative focus is the foundation of Freedom. Freedom is only possible with the responsibility of creating. Individual responsibility is the hallmark of Freedom and spiritual development. Pain and pleasure are the strongest incentives for change. The Israelites suffered immensely to arrive at this revelation. A more universal vision of strict monotheism emerged: One God for Judah and One God for all. In the streamlining of their faith, there could be no One and the many manifestations of the Creator. There must only be One God. In God's defense: The God of the Old Testament is a reflection of the violent times and the men who received His revelation. The grim repercussions for ignoring scripture mirror when Power was a justifiable means to an end. Do not make God angry. There must only be One God. The first commandment was very clear:

Thou shalt have no other gods before me.

Slavery, servitude, and exile are a horrible and tortuous penalty. Obviously, this God was serious, vengeful, jealous, and, of course, masculine. The Sky God won. Along with all the idols and gods, God lost his wife and Western culture lost a connection to the Feminine and Mother Goddess as well.

Thinking as an active force for the average human being is a relatively new ability. History details the genocide of souls who dared to question the prevailing paradigm. Most often, men were the directors of the fate of nations. The priest of this newly emerging, revolutionary doctrine of the One God got the One God part right, but in so doing totally obscured the Feminine principle in Creation. The notion of God as Masculine has dominated the religious discourse for hundreds of years.

Thinking has finally evolved to reconcile the One manifestation and the many expressions of a Being so beyond any imagination. This evolution frames the questions of what is the individual experience in a dualistic world. Who is the me and who is the Thee?

All are but parts of one stupendous whole.
Alexander Pope

In determining that the One God was solitary, Masculine, and jealous, the Feminine was cast out to fend for herself. The "she" resides in the heart and practice of the Jewish people, but Asherah was lost to history.

ISLAM

Mohammed, the founder of Islam, the sister to the Judo-Christian tradition, also proclaims One god. Allah is the name of this masculine-dominated faith for whom I have found no Feminine principle. Allah, he taught, was infinitely indefinable. So much so that he forbade the artistic representations of either male, female, or animal altogether because of the tendency in the human soul to create idols, and kings (more recently, presidents, and rock stars, too). Mohammed instructed his followers on the path of spiritual perfection by adhering to dietary mandates and strict spiritual practices. This adherence to spiritual and mental disciplines gave the world a great body of scientific work as well as magnificent art and architecture. However, in this case, the foundation of a One and only God has been translated to mean the supremacy of a Power beyond comprehension. Allah is the One and only God to whom His faithful must submit.

There was a time when Islamic culture spread throughout the Mediterranean, the Middle East, and into China. The early Muslims were merchants who traveled extensively. They encountered the great works of Aristotle and the scientific wonders of China. There were no prohibitions to knowledge and the faith prospered. Without the constraints of superstition, wisdom, and knowledge flourished to give the world such great advances in higher math such as algebra, trigonometry, and the understanding of the cipher devised in India that led to the decimal system. Arabic numbers replaced Roman numerals changing calculation altogether. Muslim scientists studied the refraction of sunlight in raindrops and offered an explanation of primary and secondary rainbows. They studied mechanics, the camera obscura, and paper-making. The Golden Age of Islamic culture took place between 750-1258 AD when Baghdad was a cultural center of civilization where wise men gathered to learn.

What caused the demise of such a brilliant culture? What forces were at work that seems to have arrested its development at the height of its influence? Some scholars speculate that there were economic failures that affected cultural life. Others look to another tendency of the human soul. At a point in the expansion of learning, the prevailing paradigm began to perpetuate itself. *Ijtihad,* individual learning, and research were abandoned in favor of *tagleed,* or institutionalized thought born out of imitation and repetition of what built the culture. The doctrine that destiny supersedes thought and Allah alone was Truth froze an evolution towards the sanctity of the individual. Islam has no child upon the knee of its mother. An individual's success is predicated solely on the blessing of Allah because if success depended merely upon one's personal struggle, then everyone in the world would be successful. Struggle is predestined by Allah alone.

The Koran, as the word of Mohammed, has been codified in the institution of Sharia Law which dictates moral and religious behavior. There is no separation of religion and state affairs. Sharia Law is determined by the consensus of religious scholars who have the authority to judge secular crime, politics, and economic issues. Within the faith there are the modernists, the traditionalists, and the fundamentalists who may interpret Mohammed's intentions in entirely different extremes. How Sharia Law is executed within its cultural boundaries is up to the men doing the interpretation. Women may have been a part of the Golden Era, but are now subject to religious laws that prohibit their participation in their society. According to Sharia Law, a family even has the right to execute a woman to restore the family's honor. Women have been stoned and beaten with chains for not complying with this political regime. In 2011 a woman accused of adultery was sentenced to death by stoning. The worldwide outcry was so loud that her sentence was commuted to death by hanging. This is hardly an isolated incident. In many cases, a woman's status is equivalent to that of her father's or husband's livestock. Women have no legal rights, can't own property, and are still used as political pawns. Although, Islam is the fastest-growing religion in the United States, many of us in the West have difficulty understanding this faith that appears to be so totally patriarchal, especially in the Middle East where women live behind a veil and have little to say. The male- controlled civilization leaves little margin for the individual to progress beyond the scope of the religious freedom of the Middle Ages.

The revelation of individual experience is sacred. It takes artistry and strength of character to maintain two opposing points of view to arrive at a perception free of sympathy or antipathy. Being able to transcend appearances to arrive at essence is the hallmark of advanced thought. Buddha called the Way the Middle Path and American Indians refer to the Good Red Road. Christians refer to the need to take up your cross and follow Christ. Each of the above disciplines requires the seeker to find his or her place on the continuum of duality; if adherence to either polarity prevails, only half of the Truth can be revealed. Reconciliation of opposites is mandatory for an individual in search of a personal Truth.

CHRISTIANITY

Christianity spread westward. It did not encounter the rich cultural influence that Islam found in the philosophy of Aristotle or the wisdom of China. Christianity met superstitions that made investigations into the nature of the known world and other philosophies punishable by death, exile, and torture. The pervading customs of the Celts and tribes they encountered were so deeply pagan and superstitious that fear of them isolated basic Christian doctrine safely behind cloister walls. However, within the faith, there were few prohibitions to limit artistic representation of Creation or Its Creator. The art of the early Christian church was deeply religious and through the Catholic Church, the image of Jesus, Mary, and the Holy Spirit flourished. Angels and cherubs fluttered in adoration. Mary was the intercessor and petitioner to a greater authority who may not have been so inclined to listen.

Not all of the doctrines we attribute to Christianity today were fostered during the life of Jesus Christ. The center of Christianity was in Constantinople during the time of the Emperor Constantine. The Emperor convoked the First Council of Nicaea in the second century to decide on basic declarations of faith and codify divisions in how Christianity was taught. His interest in calling the conference was not so much to catalyze the emerging faith, but to unify the Roman Empire. The biggest issue was the dual nature of Jesus and the establishment of his divinity. Was Jesus created or begotten? Within this debate was the status of Mary, the mother of Jesus. Politics were no different than they are today. Men were exiled and excommunicated because their views challenged the prevailing doctrines.

After much debate, the First Council established the divinity of Jesus and the date of Easter. However, these early Christians adopted many of the attitudes of their Hebrew for- fathers, especially regarding women. The books of *Genesis, Exodus, Leviticus,* and *Numbers* set a tone for the treatment of women that prevailed then, prevails in Islam, and defines many of the Christian values some faiths profess today. Tertullian, an early church father, wrote: *You (women) are the devil's gateway: you are the unsealer of that (forbidden) tree: you are the first deserter of the divine law: you are she who persuaded him whom the devil was not valiant enough to attack. You destroyed so easily God's image, man. On account of your desert- that is, death-even the Son of God had to die.*

Even the reformer, John Calvin, continued by stating: *Woman is more guilty than a man, because she was seduced by Satan, and so diverted her husband from obedience to God that she was an instrument of death leading to all perdition. It is necessary that a woman recognize this, and that she learns to what she is subjected; and not only against her husband. This is reason enough why today she is placed below and that she bears within her ignominy and shame.*

These beliefs about the nature of womankind have persisted to the present day. "His" story has obscured the sacred nature of all human beings. The great mystery of life is in the co- creation of life. It is a powerful force that cannot be rationally controlled. Along with doctrines of divinity, the First Council banned self-castration by holy men. No wonder the mermaid as the Feminine was blamed for the struggles the pious encountered.

The early fathers ruled on many divisive matters that ultimately split the church East and West. The Trinity became doctrine in 360 AD. The Catholic Church incorporated the Father, Son, and Holy Spirit into God in three blessed persons. Not all Early Christians subscribed to the imagination because of the same problem the Hebrews encountered in the imagination of a One God. How could there be three operative principles in One? Did this appear too much like a polytheistic doctrine sneaking into Christianity? There is a scripture that supports God as three in one, but factions have split on just this point because the more orthodox felt the symbology of the Trinity was pagan. The One and the Many expressions of the Almighty is a mystery that persists today.

By the fourth century AD, the men of the church had suffered through schisms of faith to establish doctrines that would continue to be points of debate even into the 21st century. This is the Church that has brought Christianity into the modern arena with such doctrines as literal translations of the Bible, heretics burning at the stake, an infallible pope, celibate priests, the Inquisition, excommunication, papal bulls, imposed birth control, and exclusion of women in the priesthood. The women of the early Christian church would, like the early Muslim women, be shocked by the exclusion of women in today's religious life.

Pure essence and pure matter, and the two joined into one were shot forth without flaw, like three bright arrows from a three string bow.
Dante

I, personally, take no issue with three principles functioning as One living process. The discussion throughout *The Mermaid's Tale* of the All being perceived in a dualistic world brings about the multiple manifestations of the One. A focus generates a unified field of consciousness, a zero-point field that is not exactly energy or empty space. God is consciousness. Even describing God as the water cycle that materializes, condenses, sleets, snows, and then rains down blessings on earth sounds more enlightened than believing that God is solely an old man on a throne. But I do take issue that the Trinity as such, is taught as though all three principles of the Trinity are Masculine. Where is the respect, reverence, and awe of the creative presence of the Feminine? In most churches across the United States, it would be blasphemous to suggest that the Feminine principle was a part of the Holy Trinity. History has been authored by a male-dominated intellect. How would life on earth have progressed if both the males and females had been educated to be equally significant to their community? What if teachers were paid as much as football players?

It is Unity that doth enchant me.
Giordano Bruno

MERMAID TALE

In the West, the Virgin Mary has survived as the sole representative of the Sacred Feminine. Her presence is undeniable to those who reverently seek her counsel and intercession; she appears to the faithful with her message of compassion and faith in the power of a living God. She assures us that God will listen to all our prayers. She is the Virgin of Guadalupe who cares for the dispossessed and marginalized; grottos dedicated to her apparitions and her message are located all over the world in some of the most unsuspecting locations. She still inspires schools, churches, and the merciful to care for the less fortunate. She could be the voice of splashing waters or the presence of the Holy Spirit who comforts and protects. However, my mother warned me against my Catholic neighbors who, she said, tolerated idols and worshiped Mary.

For all of us who have emerged from the mythological and frothy waters of the subconscious, the name Mary represents the emergence of the Feminine influence on worldly evolution. A casual read of the New Testament, however, reveals not one, not two, but five Marys who played a significant role in the life of Jesus.

Mary, the mother of Jesus, was no ordinary woman. She was born into a faith that anticipated and prepared for millennia for the birth of the Messiah who would redeem humanity. To this end, daily affairs were arranged to maximize the viability of the community, body, and soul to nurture such a Being. Mary was chosen for this assignment because she was the result of evolution towards this perfection.

Here is where the story gets interesting in the connection of Mary to the feminine and how her name reflects our fish-tailed maven. Mary, or Maria, comes from the Latin *mare*-or the sea. The sea as an archetype echoes the emerging of consciousness and connects us to the story of Jesus. He is, after all, the fisher of men. The symbol most Christians believe to be a fish, was used extensively as a secret revelation of Christian society. When drawn, the symbol appears as an embrace, but also a net that connects the believers into one community. The symbol reminds us of the promise that Jesus made "Where two or more are gathered together, there am I also." Could it be two circles interlocking—the center of one circle becomes the periphery of the other, meaning that when two become one, a third, or middle kingdom, can be created wherein dwells the Holy Spirit or the Land of Heart's Desire?

We can make further connections between the sea of myth and legend and biblical Marys. Many of us have come to know the other Mary as Mary Magdalene, not the harlot of the New Testament, but as a woman who had a significant relationship with Jesus. Research connecting Mary Magdalene to Jesus in this manner is easy to find. *The Golden Legend*, written 1260-1275, is a medieval book that ties this Mary even closer to the mystery of the sea. This story tells how three women named Mary sought exile in France. The people of the seaside town of Saintes-Maries-de-la-Mer claim is where Mary Magdalene, Mary Saloma, the mother of John the Apostle, and Mary the wife of Cleophas arrived with a child of Mary Magdalene and Jesus.

For the sake of a good story, we can further link the mermaid to this royal line of French Kings. These kings claim they are, in fact, the guardians of the Grail. The Mer in Merovingian is for the sea as it was for Mary. Sirens enhance the Merovingian coat of arms and allude that there was a mermaid in their ancestral past. Melusine or Mary, the mermaid remains an active archetype in our psyche.

The Blessed Mother may also play a major role and be the principle on which the sacrament of marriage was based. This sacrament blesses the union of two people, presumably Masculine and Feminine archetypes. Marriage is the foundation of culture because the initiation demands the refining of each partner in love. This stabilizing union allows for something much greater to take place in a society. In marriage, the vesica piscis becomes the real-life illustration of the transforming power of Love. Within the institution of marriage, one can be instructed in the invisible art of how to create a sacred place into which the spirit of love can reside. Marriage creates a chosen periphery of experience, and because the resolve is made, other powers rush to grow a life that is the product of one plus one, which equals more than can be calculated. Certainly, within marriage, the family, home, children, and community become the direct revelation of the integrity of the ability to create a sacred space, but only when both partners participate equally.

Mary has inspired the building of cathedrals, artistic masterpieces, and music that can bring tears even to the non-believer. In Mary, the notion that women have a major role in creation has been kept alive.

First we have to believe, and then we believe.
—G.C. Lichenberg

The Catholic Church was quick to Christianize sacred sites of the pagan tribes it encountered. Zennor is a coastal village in Cornwall, England. Here on the cliffs overlooking the Atlantic Ocean is such a site built on what in 600 AD was Celtic. Today, the chapel bears the name of a Christian saint, but it was once visited by the locals for its healing water and venerated for the mermaid who lived in a neighboring cove. The legend tells us that this mermaid became enchanted with the voice of Matthew, a young man who sang the closing hymn every night. Our mermaid dressed herself in a long gown to cover her tail and slowly made her way to the coastal promontory to listen to his song. The bolder she got, the longer she stayed; she stayed and fell in love, but she knew if she did not return to the sea, she would perish. Matthew fell in love as well. He carried her to the sea one night where he followed her beneath the waves. He was never seen again. The villagers will tell you if you listen closely before the sunset, Matthew's song may come lilting on the evening air. Even in the wake of Christian zeal a vestige of the mermaid continues in two remaining bench ends that are carved to portray the Mermaid of Zennor.

What is this powerful hold the mermaid and sea have on our imagination? She is the Feminine that so seduces us to believe in the unseen forces of Nature and tempts us to dissolve back into a past that no longer exists. *She* may have been written out of history, tangled up in the subconscious of men, marginalized, excommunicated, burned at the stake, or tried for witchcraft, but *she* has survived. For the most part, Western culture has failed to go beyond her beautiful countenance to tap into the transformative qualities that lie deep in the subconscious and close to each person's heart. These powerful qualities are never dormant. The Feminine countenance of God may have appeared passive in the past. The transformation of culture we are witnessing today is taking place because her faithful are listening to what she has to say. Although, suggesting the presence of a Feminine presence in Christianity is still considered blasphemous, a new world is beginning to emerge; a new world can be born through the conscious efforts of humankind.

Some day after mastering the winds, the tides and gravity, we shall harness for God the energies of love, and then for the second time in history of the world, man will have discovered fire.
—Teilhard de Chardan

MY MERMAID LINE

I came from a long line of sea maidens. My mother's name was Nina, though, most likely, not a daughter of Damkina. She was a mermaid coaxed to the shore by promises of true love in exchange for a world that on the single side of the veil had no meaning for women in the 1940s. Marriage was the societal expectation and how women found credibility in a man's world. As an interesting caveat, until the 1950s, an astrologer would look at the tenth house of a woman's astrological chart to determine what her husband's (and not her) work in the world would be.

For sixty-plus years, my mother served this ideal. However, in her last years, the frustrations and anger came out as temper tantrums and skin rashes that betrayed how deeply she had hidden her secret Self. I arrived at her bedside minutes before she was finally released back into the great ocean of time. I miss her now more than ever.

She had not been alone on the outskirts of her life. My college roommate's mother suffered multiple sessions of electric shock treatments to help her cope. A general's wife next door drank scotch, and when there was no scotch, she downed a bottle of vanilla extract. Today, antidepressants obscure the neurosis. My mother willingly performed her duties. She bathed, dressed, and had a sit-down dinner ready at 6:45 p.m. every night when my father came home; she could have been the cover girl for a *Good Housekeeping* article of the 1950s. She stood behind him and, like many a wife of the Greatest Generation, helped to make men, like my dad, who saved the world. These wives and mothers of the '50s were their own army, dressed in cocktail gowns, and long white gloves, and held together with Playtex foundation garments.

Everyone in the family had a role, and I had to keep it a secret when I deviated from those expectations. The price for not keeping up appearances was the brunt of the colonel's anger. My father's temper was a tactic he used to maintain control. This is the legacy of a lopsided evolution where anger prevailed and men were rewarded for being the aggressor; they, however, were and are victims of this Feminine-less paradigm as well.

We feel nameless and empty when we forget our stories,
leave our heroes unsung, and ignore the rites
that mark our passage from one stage to another.
—Sam Keen

Looking back, I found my parents' behavior disconcerting. Like a good soldier, I tried to adhere to the family plan. I ventured out to try some version of myself only to be shocked or overwhelmed by the forces at work on dry land. I tried to grow up to be the colonel's wife I was raised to be, but the only thing I did learn was how to give a good party, and that alcohol helped to dissolve social awkwardness. I wasn't a classic beauty by any means, but even so, I was confused by the attention my face and body brought me. I actually thought boys liked me for *me*, for the intelligent, funny, and compassionate person I thought I was. However, I soon learned to play the game of listening, smiling, and clever, but not too intelligent, conversation. To the world, I was only what I looked like. No one saw the real me. The real me was invisible. Patterns of invisibility persisted into my adult life, but I haven't forgotten the secrets whispered to me at birth. I have held onto a promise of purpose and promised myself that I would not forget.

I won't forget, I won't forget, I won't forget. And, I haven't forgotten. On the surface, I have done my duties. I suffered from a sort of personality dyslexia. I was mired in a distorted image of what I looked like, always on the outside of myself, looking back—comparing and judging, eating too much or not enough, unable to keep food down. I was told, "Just swallow it," by my well-meaning mother. It was how she coped. Secretly, in my heart of hearts, I have been putting together a puzzle, mining the depths of my experience armed only with the gifts my mother left me: a good sense of humor, a love of pretty things, and a belief that affairs of the heart are sacred. It has been an emotional rodeo, bucking bull. I refused to eat the baloney, and have arrived alive and grateful.

A Hebrew myth tells us that when a child is born, an angel takes it under his wing and recites the Torah to it. Having done that, he puts his forefinger on the infant lip and says one word, "Forget!" Clearly, every tradition has a similar angel, for where is the human creature who lacks that indentation of the upper lip, the little valley of flesh where the same word has been so ineffaceable impressed? And, indeed, of necessity. For how, without forgetting, can remembering arise? And remembering leads to search."
——from Remembering, by P.L. Travers
Parabola Summer 1991

The world is in great need of the Feminine to awaken to her creative duties. She is the voice of conscience that speaks softly to all mermaids and mermen. She seems to say, "Lose your tail—become human. Create a new human story. Do not faint is the face of a challenge. *This time you are the chalice, and the Elixir of Life is the potion of your becoming.*"

Acknowledging the value of the whispering soul is just the beginning. This is the next greatest transformation the human race will go through. This transformation will bring us to the brink of metamorphosis when the invisible soul's capacities of awe, wonder, and imagination join respectfully with clear thinking based on experience. It will be a new basis for exploring a multi- dimensional reality.

The merfolk, for there are both merman and mermaids, are like the pollywogs of the human species. We both have to transform our tail (and our tale) to grow into an ever-expanding definition of what it means to be human. The limitations are to be found in the dark places of our thinking, where the dragon resides.

Know this:
Dragons guard a treasure.

CHAPTER 3

Dragons Be Here

Dragons and mermaids were depicted on seafaring charts to warn of the dangers of uncharted waters. These magical beasts became synonymous with the primal forces of Nature that the adventurous soul would encounter in its search for the unknown. The consequences of such a meeting varied depending on who was telling the story and in which hemisphere the tale was told. Descriptions could be totally opposite when describing attitude, anatomy, and symbolism.

The Chinese people consider themselves to be the descendants of dragons. These powerful creatures command respect as they bestow health, wealth, and wisdom. The Chinese word for dragon has the onomatopoeic quality of the sound of *thunder*. A dragon could be a shape-shifter, appearing human with the powers of speech. Dragons were wise above all other creatures, and so of course, the Emperor was considered the Head Dragon. The benevolent dragon of the East dances in parades to bless the land with good fortune. Quan Yin, the Oriental Goddess of Compassion, is frequently depicted astride a dragon as if the beast were a trusted companion. She carries a pearl of wisdom in one hand and a vial of human tears in the other.

The Western dragon, on the other hand, is regarded as a formidable opponent. It is a much darker, greedier beast. Before the eighteenth century, the Western dragon was considered more real than mythological. It could have been any large serpent or monstrous foe. The Persian word for the beast alludes to the one who has ten thousand horses—a force to be contended with for sure. The Greek word for dragon arose from the verb "to see clearly," or "one with the deadly glance." Dragons, therefore, adorned scabbards and prows of ships bound for battle.

The Greek constellation of Draco is a dragon that wraps itself closely around the North Star; all the other constellations hang from it in the night sky. The Romans associated the dragon with all of the mysteries of the earth. The Western dragon, however, has malevolent overtones; its lair is deep in the earth in underground caves. The King James Version of the Bible equated this treacherous creature with the serpent and made it interchangeable with the Devil and instinctual, irrational fear.

The dragon resides in the unexplored arenas of our psyche, on the periphery of our experience. These furious beasts guard the territories of the unexplained, untrodden paths. They are guardians on the threshold of experience, staking claim to hordes of stolen treasure. Unappeased, they breathe fire and belch smoke that pollutes the air, while their blood pollutes the wilderness. They demand the sacrifice of the innocent or they pledge to lay waste to nations.

There is a sense of gathering gloom, an unknowing that the neophyte on the path experiences when she reaches or is propelled beyond the periphery of her experience—here is deep water. Unassisted, the Darkness sets in, and one finds out what one is made of.

Saint George is the patron saint of England. This dragon slaying story is celebrated once a year on September 29; the festival falls just after the autumnal equinox, when the balance of sun forces begins to diminish, summer fades, and we look forward to the coming darkness of winter. It is our story and the story of the emerging Self.

The story begins with a kingdom terrorized by a terrible dragon's appetite for innocent young maidens. The village people must regularly draw straws to choose whose daughter will be the next sacrificial virgin. When all of the village virgins have been sacrificed, the king's only daughter, who up until now had been exempt from the lottery, must be taken beyond the city walls to meet her doom. At the last moments of her life, Sir George appears. He prays, and the archangel Michael (who is himself the countenance of Christ) appears—not to fight the battle for him, but to give him the courage to do battle against the dragon and free the maiden. He does, is canonized, and is so celebrated on Michaelmas every year.

The story is about how we sell out to our fear, compromise, and diminish our soul, and the soul of our kingdom. It recognizes that meaningful fights require courage and that we have backup whenever we realize that we are above our heads, or if we ourselves are incapable of fighting a formidable foe. Uncharted realms, darkness, and thresholds of experience demand that we reinvent who we thought we were, and in so doing, reach out to powers of transformation not available to us in normal waking consciousness. It is not only possible, but critical, for each person to find the courage to meet the darkness, dragon, and evil of his or her own creation.

The salient point of debate concerning the fight of any formidable opponent is whether or not to brandish a sword, courting the consequence of not knowing how many heads will regenerate from a beheading, or taming it in such a way to put the forces to work in the service of humanity. In either case, I believe it best to feed the lamb and starve the wolf. The dragon of the West taunts the courageous or foolhardy to, "Come and get me."

IT TAKES TWO

If you do not know essence and don't know life, you will split the creative and receptive into two paths. But the day you join them together to form the elixir, you fall drunken into the jug, yet have no need of support.
—Tan Guangzhen, Chinese philosopher

The three-dimensional world that we first wake up to is dualistic in nature. Generally speaking, perception is spoken in bursts of, "I love it!" or, "Oooh, I hate it! It's so %##@!" It is an either/or montage of black-and-white opinions. Most often, it is easier to know what we do not like than to know the subtle nuances that bring us joy. Negativity mesmerizes thinking and cripples action. Creation is set up in basic dualistic terms to give parameters to an archetype, but neither of the extremes is capable of defining an absolute.

Everything that originated from the
tree of knowledge carries in it duality.
—Zohar, mystical Jewish text

The essence of the ancient teachings of the alchemists can be simply drawn as two separate symbols—one with arrows raying out and one with arrows raying in. Although these symbols appear as a polarity, they establish a point and periphery of experience. Integrity of point and periphery is necessary to avoid collapse of consciousness. Point and periphery are central to the understanding of the mysterious relationships between contracting and expanding, exhaling and inhaling, and waking and sleeping, yes and no.

The still point of turning is being one with essence.
At the still point, there the dance is.
Except for the point, the still point,
there would be no dance, and there is only one dance.
—T.S. Eliot

Periphery is the perceived limit of understanding or interaction. Understanding can be enlarged through study and practice. If I follow my curiosity further than I am able to personally integrate, a collapse occurs. This creative tension honors both the point and periphery to determine the boundary of limitation or capacity to understand.

A human being is a part of the whole, called by us the "Universe," a
part limited in time and space. He experiences himself, his thought,
and feelings as something separated from the rest—a kind of optical
delusion of his consciousness. This delusion is a kind of prison for us, restricting
us to our personal desires and to affection for a few
persons nearest to us. Our task must be to free ourselves from this
prison by widening our circle of compassion to embrace all living creatures and
whole of nature in its beauty. Nobody is able to
achieve this completely, but the striving for such achievement is in
itself a part of the liberation and foundation for inner security.
—Albert Einstein

The whole wide world is only he and she.
—Sri Aurobindo Ghose

Spanish designates gender through the spelling of a word. Everything is either male or female, right down to horse or house or dog and doll—el caballo or la casa, el perro or la muñeca. Spanish recognizes that there is something inherently male or female in its naming. Nouns are imbued with a soul-life that we do not experience in English. English obscures subtlety in a rush to intellectualize or capture consciousness in a purely materialistic approach to life.

That being said, the nature of the natural world is to manifest itself in terms of duality, even if English has obscured the inherent gendered overtones that create the tension of consciousness. Even so, I believe we could all agree that the following words could be identified along gender lines:

affection	sex
anabolic	catabolic
black	white
clothes	cars
curved	straight
invisible	visible
left	right
listen	talk
manipulative	aggressive
moon	sun
multi-task	single task
my fault	your fault
naïve	cynical
nature	man
ours	mine
passive	active
picture think-ing	linear think-ing
soft	hard
sympathy	antipathy
unconditional	conditional
prey	predator

A central precept of a Chinese worldview finds its expression in the *Tai jih*, or the classic symbol, *yin and yang*. The Tai jih is symbolic of a Chinese awareness that seemingly contrary expressions exist in a continuum of interdependency and have no true value in isolation. What does it mean to be hot without something cold to act as a point of comparison? The awareness of the connectedness of polar opposites is fundamental in Chinese philosophy, science, and medicine. Yin and yang are not static, but each has an eternal sense of cosmic ebb and flow to include two aspects in a single reality. As the symbol—half black, half white—each has the seed of the other within itself. Common usage has tried to cast this dynamic duo in terms of morality, good and bad. However, a Taoist practitioner discounts the notion of an ultimate good or bad.

The symbol takes its form from complex images and thoughts of the I Ching, known through hexagrams or trigrams. The *I Ching*, also called *The Book of Changes*, depicts circumstances in a continual state of metamorphosis, or ebb and flow, represented in picture form. Yin and Yang are manifestations of Light and Darkness and are depicted as having to do with the sun's movement across the sky. Yin is the shady place on the north slope of a mountain, while yang is the sunny side exposure. The yin and yang is an active symbol revealing that the obscured will be revealed, and what appears in the full light of understanding will, over time, be obscured.

Let us learn to appreciate that there will be a time
When trees are bare, and look forward to the time
when we may pick the fruit.
-Checkov

Yin is slow, soft, yielding, diffuse, cold, wet, passive, water, earth, moon, femininity, and nighttime. Yang, by contrast, is fast, hard, aggressive, fire, sky, sun, masculinity, and daytime. Through the I Ching, confrontation manifests in terms of engagement or defense and can be resolved through principles of attack and stillness.

All existing things are really one.
We regard those that are beautiful and rare as valuable,
and those that are ugly as foul and rotten.
The foul and rotten may come to be transformed
into what is rare and valuable,
and the rare and valuable into what is foul and rotten.
—Chuang Tzu

We can examine the Darkness, or Yin, with a sixth-grade physics experiment. The experiment requires a room to be prepared in such a way that no Light can penetrate into the desired Darkness. I arrived at the classroom Sunday afternoon with duct tape, tarps, and heavy black plastic to do battle with the Light. I soon realized I was up against a formidable foe. Phase one was tedious and required help from my essential assistant, my husband. Once the doors and windows were taped shut and plastic draped over them, we turned off the lights to survey our work. Our hard work was an apparent success and would have remained such had we left immediately.

One loses a sense of Self and awareness of one's surroundings without the benefit of Light. Initially, the room was only filled with Darkness. Without the benefit of any light, it was impossible to make out anything other than my own thoughts. Lingering longer, however, it became apparent that the battle for dominance was not over. Darkness gave way as Light found its way through the smallest pinprick of a hole to reveal forms in the room cloaked in a spectrum of grays. Each time one avenue of illumination was blocked, the pupil of my eye dilated further to allow me to see further and further into the Darkness. What was obscured began to give way to reveal another reality once hidden from view. Although I lost the individualizing experience of Color, I was amazed at the black-and-white world that existed parallel to my daylight reality. This Darkness did not overwhelm me, nor was I incapacitated. Certainly, the loss of Color diminished the quality of the experience, but I encountered an ability to perceive beyond my initial perception. The longer I remained visually isolated, the more the pupil of my eye dilated to redefine the nature of Darkness. More remarkable still was how persistent the Light was.

> *The function of darkness is to open the pupil to the Light.*
> *SDL*

We carry a bit of the Darkness with us attached to the heel of our foot wherever we go to remind us there is a shadow side to all matter. This shadow may look benign enough, but the shadow of our being is an active force that brings us to face what was untraceable. It is a result of the many decisions we make to either omit or include things in our life. The Catholic Church calls them sins of omission, or carnal sins.

> *Everything that originated from the tree of knowledge*
> *carries in it duality.*
> *-Zohar, mystical Jewish text*

Jung calls this phenomenon the *shadow*. Rudolf Steiner's name for it is the dubleganer or the *double*. The influence of this *double* is very real and directly related in intensity to the energy the person exerts to suppress it. Steiner describes the *double* as an actual energy of being that can and does manipulate reality to reveal our unconscious wishes and desires. It is a repository for aspects of the Self one does not want to acknowledge. Nothing is hidden that will not be revealed in time. There are no secret conversations that take place where no one can hear. Nor are there indiscretions that are guiltily performed when no one is looking. The *double* is active below the surface of awareness, always watching because it never sleeps. As the *double* is confronted, character is defined.

> *I have a little shadow that goes in and out with me,*
> *and what can be the use of him is more than I can see.*
> —*Robert Louis Stevenson*

The physical body has a visceral response whenever the Double exerts its presence. It may rear its ugly head when someone or something challenges or threatens a pet premise. I can feel something rise up in me that I experience as so self- righteous; the tone of my voice can even change. What happens to you? Squeeze a dish rag and water comes out, squeeze an orange, and orange juice comes out. What comes out of us when we are pressed or stressed?

Rudolf Steiner, in his work, *Geographic Medicine: The Secret of the Double*, describes how the *double* is intensified by the electrical magnetic fields of mountains, especially those running north and south, like the Sierra Nevada. The European mountain ranges that run east and west do not exacerbate the *double* in nearly the same way. The *double* is a product of one's earthly Life, and so cannot pass through the gates of death, but awaits the soul in its next incarnation. Families can share *doubles* and tragically, an adult perpetuates the sinful drama onto the soul of a young child who gets blamed or shamed for a parent's anger, or misfortune. The shadow falls across the face of innocence, obscuring enchantment and revealing a purely materialistic world. This is the cave of Darkness, in which the personal dragon lives.

> *Everybody's shouting, "Which side are you on?"*
> —*Bob Dylan*

EVIL IS A FORM OF SPIRITUAL DYSLEXIA

Evil is a symptom of a spiritual learning disability. It is the result of a lack of courage, vision, understanding, or vocabulary to keep a soul from a collapse of consciousness in the face of the unknown. Evil is perpetuated in misunderstandings, resulting in a lack of *I sight*. We in the West are ambivalent about evil. The institutional Christian church makes Darkness and evil synonymous with the ultimate bogeyman. The Devil lurks behind the unknown to rob the faithful of their heavenly real estate. The Devil is blamed for all the bad in the world, while the naïve ask why God would allow such atrocities. The English language demonstrates that we are more acquainted with the various nuances of money, power, and technology than we are with this formable architect of destiny.

Darkness cannot drive out darkness: only light can do that.
Hate cannot drive out hate, only love can do that.
—Martin Luther King Jr.

Knowing and naming are tools of consciousness. Language not only reflects a culture's worldview but also helps to define it. The Chinese language had no word for science until 1993, and it now has a vocabulary to rival any Western technology. The Chinese continued to invent a language in accordance with their culture's transformation. The Sami people, an indigenous circumpolar tribe, have hundreds of ways to describe snow. The Spanish have countless ways of describing the emotion of attraction. In English: love. In Spanish: Amar is the strongest expression; Querer is the most common; Adorar has religious connotations; Exaltar is religiously inclined; Enamorar is a love very strongly expressed; Gustar is an attraction; Estimar denotes a respectful friendship; Apreciar and Apegar describe a friendship, and Afetar is used to speak of a fondness of an object. Additionally, the language has built into it expressions of fondness that separate the dearness of a single relationship from the civility to the masses.

Webster's Dictionary does not offer significant insight into the nature of evil that battles for the human heart. The definition is so broad and certainly does not define the forces that manipulate consciousness and polarize communities. Evil, it states, must show the intention of causing harm or destruction. Evil deliberately violates some moral code. Societies have moral codes: not so much as distinctions of good and bad, but to protect the individual and her society from the sorrow, distress, and calamity that arise from actual or imputed bad character or conduct. Evil has become synonymous with grievous, monstrous, black, dark, sinister, immoral, or demonic. Simply stated, God is the source of all wisdom, justice, and goodness, but the purpose of evil is to seduce or corrupt the human being.

Christian Scientists believe that evil is the result of misunderstanding and perceptions that lead to incorrect choices. Mormons state that evil keeps us from discovering the nature of God. The Koran would lead us to believe that evil is not a cause, but a result. God is good, but men do evil. Thomas Aquinas describes evil as the absence of God and the result of lies and deceit. In the drive to convert the wicked and protect the saved, the church of the eighteenth century cast evil as extreme moral wickedness, and proclaimed that evildoers would be cast into a pit of everlasting fire. Through such encounters that define character we may come to understand that, in fact, when properly understood or digested, EVIL is LIVE spelled backward.

> *One might as well try to ride two horses*
> *moving in different directions,*
> *as to try to maintain in equal force two opposing*
> *or contradictory sets of desires.*
> *—Robert Collier*

There is no doubt about it that human beings have turned the world into a painful place. Evil, sorrow, distress, and calamity certainly are the result of bad behavior. We in the West would do well to have a better understanding of the forces of the invisible architect of misery.

Some of the above may scare the hell out of us, and frighten us into adhering to a moral code. I seek to tune the harp of my heart to the chord that David found to please the Lord. We might do well to take dancing lessons, but I don't think you get to dance without meeting the guardians at the threshold of duality. This is where confrontation takes place that defines who we are by the nature of choices we make in the battle of *either/or.*

> *The most valuable thing the Psalms do for me is to express*
> *the same delight in God which made David dance.*
> —C.S. Lewis

GUARDIANS

Perhaps, Rudolf Steiner's greatest contribution to spiritual science is the imagination of the Guardians of Threshold bordering upon the world known to our ordinary consciousness. These guardians are the dual faces of *Evil,* known as the fallen angels Lucifer and Ahriman. I have taken the liberty to understand these teachings using the following logic: If all creation is male and female and all things created have shadows, then the two faces of evil are a product of duality and are respectively the shadow of male and female. These are actual beings as formidable as fire and ice, as real as hysteria and despair. These creatures of Light and Darkness wreak havoc as they orchestrate obstacles to perfection. The unschooled heart is easily seduced by the charisma of one and fear of the other.

Nations have their own collective shadow that rises in conflict within itself, and one country against another, to determine just who is the strongest and most powerful. We think that actual people perpetuate battles when in effect these invisible energies have a voracious appetite for blood. They are the shadow forces that may be Feminine in one skirmish or Masculine in another. Drunk with power, the possessed seek total control while soldiers and civilizations do the bidding of these forces directing destiny.

School administrations are by nature thought-driven, and masculine in their execution of policy. Teachers are the nurturers, the celebrators of performance, selflessly working and paid less. Teaching is still considered women's work. This tendency is changing, as teachers speak out against policies that have little relevance to the role of education. At times a parent body may try to be the masculine force and demand policy changes, but more often, teachers would like to consider the parent as a nurturer and themselves as the governor of circumstance.

A similar scenario gets played out within a family. Behind closed doors, it can be revealing to see who really runs the show. Who takes on the decision making and who is subservient? Parents used to be in total control. We live in a society wherein this picture is changing. Parents seek their children's opinions in supermarkets and at bedtimes. Parenting in many cases is ineffective because of the fear that we might come off looking like all the poor examples of authority we have witnessed. Children really do not want to make all the decisions.

So here we have the two faces of the creators of circumstance that will either make us stronger or destroy the gift of humanity; the dragon. Lucifer is the shadow of the Feminine and is desirous of all things beautiful. Lucifer seeks to be adored and worshipped. Women seeking the elusive hallmark of beauty may be caught up in the quest for the next solution for disappearing chin lines or wrinkles that now obscure the beauty of innocence. The glamour of appearances or outer, material beauty, for beauty's sake, is different from the beauty and artfulness of imbuing a home with soul, an artwork with fine proportions, or the works of Nature. The soul flourishes in the presence and pursuit of True Beauty, but Beauty can be an obstacle to spiritual development as it sets limits as to what the intellect finds acceptable. Lucifer declares that spirit is its only home—the material world is Maya. In the extreme, Lucifer thrives in an undifferentiated world of obscure thoughts and vague boundaries. Lucifer would seek a life that absolves itself from worldly responsibility and incarnation where the purpose of living is to free oneself from the Wheel of Life and Death. The material world is an illusion. Let's get on with the Rapture! But you cannot hold your breath or be the victim forever. The physical awaits the loving presence of human activity. The only way out is through the world of earthly experience.

Ahriman is less well known, most likely because much of Western culture is a reflection of the purely materialistic approach to living. This fallen angel lacks creative imagination; his thoughts are mechanical, dry, and hard. Ahriman is the cold to Lucifer's warmth. He is the scoffer and scornful companion to humankind. A body becomes stiff as the life forces contract. Form is his preoccupation, and the spiritual world is an illusion. The material world is his handiwork and woe to those who tell Ahriman what to do. However, spirit must find a home.

Hollywood's world of *make-believe-this-is-how-life-is* is the playground of both the beautifully superficial and rich or the powerful and controlling. Lucifer plays a shell game of truth with the dreamer, but Ahriman's faithful think they know all the answers in a preconceived and prejudicial way. Those who create the paradigm control the spheres of thought where the real battles are waged.

Unsettling as it may be, each person's life is the battleground. We are pushed and pulled between extremes. Life doesn't begin after death with streets of gold or hundreds of virgins. Real life is happening right *now* and it demands an answer to the question, *"Who are you?"* The human heart is fashioned moment to moment with the minute expansions and contractions of everyday living. Everyone works for God, even Lucifer and Ahriman. Evil is the result of spiritual dyslexia brought about by not actually living in a life. Once inside of one's experience, evil is reversed to read *live*. If there is but One God, then everything cooperates within this measure as a function toward a unifying force much greater than the sum of its parts.

As a species, we are crossing a threshold that requires au-thenticity and if the ancient Egyptians had it right, when the Day of Judgment comes, the human heart will be weighed against the weight of a feather.

> *Ring the bells that still can ring, forget your perfect offering.*
> *There is a crack in everything. That's how the light gets in.*
> —*Leonard Cohen*

> *Watch your thoughts. They become words.*
> *Watch your words. They become deeds.*
> *Watch your deeds. They become habits.*
> *They become characters. Character is everything.*
> —*Ralph Waldo Emerson*

Sensation creates feelings, feelings create pictures, pictures create thoughts (and emotions), thoughts direct actions (moral or not), and actions create destiny. Herein resides the foundations of

Freedom; but how often do we act with deliberate intent to fashion the content of our thoughts? Eileen Hutchins, another student of Rudolf Steiner, informs us in her series of lectures dated 1940:

Thoughts control matter.
Life transforms substance.
Spirit creates power.

DELIBERATE INTENT

As a class teacher in the Waldorf system of education, teachers sometimes write stories, sometimes a poem for each child that reflects some wisdom the child could benefit from. The following are three poems and a short story I wrote for students in my class. I wrote poems as a birthday verse for each child. Every week and on the day of the week the child was born, the child recited the poem in front of the class. Each verse I carefully crafted to create a personal imagination for his or her growth.

The charioteer waits before she goes,
reins in hands, the destination known.
Ready and waiting stand the steeds-
One clarity of thought-One strength of deeds.
The steeds that pull the chariot along-
One white-One black are strong.
The charioteer must do her part.
Thought and deed need strength of heart.
-Poem for J.

A river flows from the mountain top,
it cascades over stones and rocks.
It rushes from on high to say, "
I will be, don't get in my way!"
But error and untruth abound,
and bit by bit and ground by ground,
a dam begins to grow in spite,
denying the river its earthly right.
Each twig as untruth blocks the flow,
each cause the river to move more slow.
And twig by twig creates a dam,
now there is a lake surrounded by land.
-Poem for K.

In the shadows stands the deer,
her heart beats fast, full of fear,
of what may be without,
she trusts no one because she doubts
that she can stand tooth or claw
or survive the hunter's law.
FEAR is for all greatest beast
when the fierce prey on the least.
Until we start each day brand new
and seek to find the good and true
FEAR will be the ruler here.
We'll live in the shadows like the deer.
-Poem for A

The following pedagogical story I wrote for a class of second graders, and two girls in particular. One would stomp and fuss at the slightest social antagonism. Her tears would roll down her cheeks in vain attempts to halt any perceived assault. Children can be heartless. In contrast to her antics, another girl in the class had a very different approach to adversity. When something didn't go her way, she had no apparent emotional attachment to the outcome. She met adversity with grace. The girls had many opportunities to enjoy their personal dynamics, and I hope they are both enriched for it in the long run.

DON'T LET EM GET YOUR GOAT

Deep in the Ozark Hill Country, there lived a father and a mother, and three little children. They kept their cabin neat and tidy as everything had its place. They had cats, dogs, and chickens aplenty that laid an egg every day. Above all, their most cherished possession was a herd of blue-eyed goats. What made the goats so cherished was their long, white silky coat. Twice a day the father and his children visited the goat's barn to groom each goat until its coat shone like the evening star.

Now as it happened, a grumble of trolls took up residence under a rock bridge that was within earshot of the goat barn. It took no time at all before the trolls noticed the family's daily ritual. They believed there must be something very special happening inside the barn on the hill.

Late at night when the moon was dark, after the family retired, all four trolls made their way to the barn. Even through the darkness, they could make out the shining white coats and their beautiful blue eyes trimmed with long, fair eyelashes that gazed back at them.

Filled with the desire to possess one for their very own, they carefully removed the bell from one of the goat's collars and quietly led it away. One troll stayed behind to watch what happened the following morning when the father and his children entered the barn. He chuckled to himself as he imagined their faces when they realized the mischief they were to encounter.

The sun had not been up very long and the birds were still singing their wake-up song when the father and children arrived to perform their morning ritual. They immediately knew something was amiss. The count only confirmed their fear. One adored goat was missing! The tears and lamenting began, "Our goat! Our wonderful goat! Our wonderful goat…how can this be?" And so the cries continued.

The troll was at first intrigued, but then a pleasurable warming that began in the soles of his feet like the bubbling of water just before it boiled. It bubbled up to his head filling him with such giddiness that he could hardly control himself. If he was not mistaken, he felt himself grow in size and shape.

Returning to the bridge, he recounted with such glee how the children cried and even the father wept for the missing goat. His brother trolls barely recognized him as he had obviously grown not only bigger, bigger, and bigger all around, but also, if possible, even uglier. The trolls agreed they should return to the herd that night and steal another goat. And so it went night after night.

Each morning the family team met what they feared the most when yet again another goat went missing! The trolls grew larger and larger and larger until they were a menace in the whole county and the family had few goats left.

Had the children's mother not been consulted, they might have lost every single goat. "You can cry until you no longer have a single tear, but I would suggest that you have been feeding those rascal trolls with your crying and complaining. Tomorrow, when you find yet another goat missing, try laughing in the face of your despair. Sing, dance, and see what happens.

Following good advice, the next morning they sang, danced, and laughed in the face of their dilemma. The trolls were at first shocked by the family's festive attitude. Disbelief faded to dismay as they began to undergo changes. Little by little day by day, the deliciousness of arrogance diminished; each shrunk even faster than it had grown until every troll was hardly powerful enough to now contain the stolen goats who then broke down the fences and ran home. Now there was a very good reason to celebrate and the family in the hills laughed and sang every day thereafter.

> *For where your treasure is,*
> *there will your heart be also.*
> *—Matthew 6:21*

I certainly would not want to imply that a song and laugh will banish the darkest of nights, but it might help. "In Don't Let 'em Get Your Goat," and the poetry, I found a creative resolution to a problem in the classroom. A story always works better when dealing with adversity than a direct confrontation.

> *The best thing to have up your sleeve is a funny bone.*
> *—Gary Larson, The Far Side*

The story was an artistic response to a problem, just as the song and laugh became a technique that could be applied when facing an adversary. How problems are met determines the amount of stress one decides to take on. By choosing the door with a smiley face, similar future encounters can be avoided. Artistic expression can give a voice to feelings and attitudes that could not otherwise be understood. This lesson in equanimity is extremely important in today's job market, stock market, and political arena.

We must eradicate from the soul all fear and terror
of what comes to meet us from the future.
We must look forward with absolute equanimity
to whatever comes
and we must think only that whatever comes
is given us by a world direction full of wisdom;
it is part of what we must learn in this age,
namely to act out of pure trust in the ever-present help of spiritual worlds.
Truly, nothing else will do if our courage is not to fail us.
Let us discipline our will
and let us seek the awakening from within ourselves,
every morning and every evening.
—Rudolf Steiner

CHAPTER 4

It's Been a Privilege to Serve You

All of life is an experiment.
The more experiments you make the better.
—Ralph Waldo Emerson

Many self-development gurus would have us believe that the goal of self-fulfillment is getting the material success we want. Vision boards and affirmations asserting one's intentions and worthiness form the foundation of attracting your heart's desire. While the fundamental nature of the activity works, the premise leads us to believe that getting what we desire is the goal of self- development. I would offer that if while we are minding our affirmations and watching mind movies we are not becoming more effective, compassionate, individuals, capable of meaningful connections, we are only fulfilling Phase I of our earthly curriculum.

The individual has always had to struggle to keep from being overwhelmed
by the tribe. If you try it, you' ll often be lonely and sometimes frightened.
But, no price is too high to pay for the privilege of owning yourself.
Fredrich Nietzche

Until the 1950s, some believed that babies were born blind. Researchers thought that because a baby did not focus, it could not see. Through repetition and order, the emerging being begins to make sense of her surroundings. Initial experiments of *focus* and grasp are an amazing spectacle. Waves of forgetfulness wash over her face until the intention of grasping an object is fruitfully realized. A major feat of intention, resolve and *focus* has been accomplished. Individual growth accelerates as the little scientist owns the world, bringing together the efforts of Self and world: a working relationship of right and left eye and individual *focus* is born.

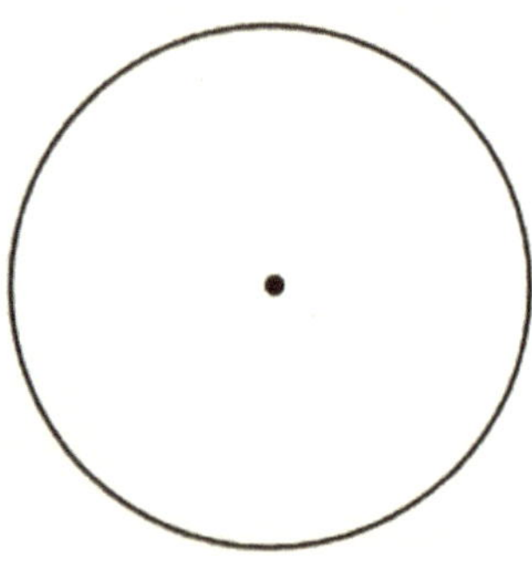

Try it for yourself. Draw a one-inch circle, placing a dot at its center. Move the circle myopically close, to within three inches of your nose. There is a distance at which the right eye reports a circle as does the left eye. With a "soft focus," you can experience a loss of a unified field of vision and with a little practice, you can bring the two circles into a unified field and then separate them into two separate circles. The phenomenon of two circles is remarkably real. The ability to focus both eyes to create an individual perspective grows over time. A unified focus is one of the hallmarks of being human, but it also hints at a much deeper mystery. An infant learns to focus her two eyes between two and three years old; in so doing, she gains a unified field of vision and arrives at the revelation of I. Eyesight and the ability to focus will play a major role in her ability to navigate obstacles and pitfalls in the material world. Most of us primarily rely on eyesight for our information. Fortunately, if one's eyesight becomes distorted, an optometrist can determine how to adjust where on the retina the image falls, and prescribe glasses to mitigate the effects of DNA and age.

As you set out in search of Ithaka,
pray that your journey be long,
full of adventures, full of awakenings,
Do not fear the adventures of old…
You will not meet them in your travels
if your thoughts are exalted and remain high,
if authentic passions stir your mind, body, and spirit.
You will not encounter fearful monsters
if you do not carry them within your soul,
if your soul does not set them up in front of you.
—Constantine Peter Cavafy

The movie *The Secret* has catalyzed a spiritual revolution. The message is that we are our thinking; it is our thinking that becomes our intentions, and it is these intentions—core beliefs— that fashion our lives. The occult wisdom of this blockbuster film doesn't expose anything new. Even though humanity as a whole has been oblivious to thinking as the leavening agent of Life, it has, nonetheless, been just as powerful in shaping individual destinies and governments. A handful of people including: dictators, kings, queens; and from the beginning of time, priests, and then the Church have directed collective thought. Throughout history, this secret ingredient has been kept from the masses. In some cases, this wisdom has been used for guidance and direction, but most often power and control. Whoever has the power wins all the money and gets to be on top.

Power is the great aphrodisiac.
—Henry Kissinger

Unlimited power is apt to corrupt the minds of those who possess it.
—William Pitt

So, if the content of our thoughts determines our experience of Life, then our thoughts are the starting point to a new tomorrow. Focusing on one's life can become a mission statement and affirmation. By doing so, you should get to something that might read:

I Am…"
I Am a child of the living God.
I Am fully awake to the possibilities that meet me every day.
I Am a co-creator of a life dedicated to my spiritual awakening.
I Am.
That's a good start.
The "I Am" is what connects and creates.
That's what Jesus said.
"I Am"…And we can do the same as well.

A point within a circle was the Egyptian, Chinese, and Mayan glyph for light. Here we see the circle with its center point as the symbol of the *"I Am,"* the One and the One—the universe and Self. How big the sphere of influence is depends on the energy created by Focus. An individual's circle expands and contracts according to the ability to focus and hold the center. Holding the center is likewise dependent on awareness at the periphery of individual experience.

Life shrinks or expands in proportion to our courage.
—Anaïs Nin

The relationship of the point to the circumference determines the congruity of the circle or the quality of refinement of the circle at its periphery. The periphery is where the Darkness resides, but where learning strategies can redefine limitation. Thinking is not just what we think about; it is equally important *how* we think. Schools don't teach them *how*—at least most don't. For thinking to be alive, it must be imbued with imagination that draws from the genius of what it means to be human. Education has changed very little since its purpose was to educate people to fit into an industrial society. The idea that people are individuals who can and should think for themselves is a relatively new concept. Today, textbooks teach what has already been taught. *Who* or *what* informs your thinking is of great consequence.

> *You give birth to that to which you fix your mind.*
> —Antoine Saint-Exupery, *The Little Prince*

Life happens on this outer edge of our experience, where we are most fresh: growing and vulnerable. The periphery is where we feel most alive—a scary premise for many who turn to pills and alcohol for relief. I postulate that this periphery of experience is the new frontier, created by one's eyesight and *I sight*. This new frontier is the undocumented universe just outside of my grasp. The new world is the uncharted territory between you and the world and between you and me.

> *If we think about it, we find that our life consists in achieving a pure relationship between ourselves and the living universe about us. This is how I save my soul by accomplishing a pure relationship between me and another person, me and a nation, me and a race of people, me and trees or flowers, me and the earth, me and the skies and sun and stars, me and the moon, an infinity of pure relationships big and little, this, if we know it, is our life and our eternity; the subtle perfected relation between me and the circumambient universe.*
> —D.H. Lawrence

SACRED GEOMETRY

Pythagoras initiated his students into the sacred blueprint of creation called Sacred Geometry; it reveals an intelligent matrix behind all manifested forms and its relationship to the underlying Oneness. Sacred Geometry demonstrates that Creation is more than the sum of its parts. All things appear to emerge out of geometric codes as expressed in snowflakes, the branching of trees, the cornea of the eye, a sunflower, and strands of DNA. From the finite to the infinite form follows geometric archetypes.

> *Nature geometrizes universally in all her manifestations.*
> *H.P. Blavaksky*

Sacred Geometry as a mathematical science illustrates how form is generated in the physical world. Straight and curved lines form the fundamental language of the computer world, similar to the binary system's 1s and 0s. The circle is the primary symbol that encompasses *everything*; it is also descriptive of each *individual.* It's a primal conundrum of One and one. It is the seed in which all things are possible.

> *As the web issues from the spider, as little sparks proceed*
> *from fire, so from the one soul proceeds all breathing*
> *animals, all worlds, all gods, and all beings.*
> *—Brohad-Aranyaka, Hindu scripture*

The natural world is born through the awareness of all things *other*, and then finding one's place in the spectrum of possibilities. The mystery of the ages, the mystery of creation and regeneration, resides in the resolution of how one organizes into evermore sophisticated or differentiated consciousnesses to become two and three and more:

There are only two ways to live life.
One is as though nothing is a miracle.
The other is as though everything is a miracle.
—Albert Einstein

VESICA PISCIS

The vesica piscis is formed by the common area created by two identical circles with the center of circle B being on the circumference of circle A. The vesica piscis is this common ground and shared vision.

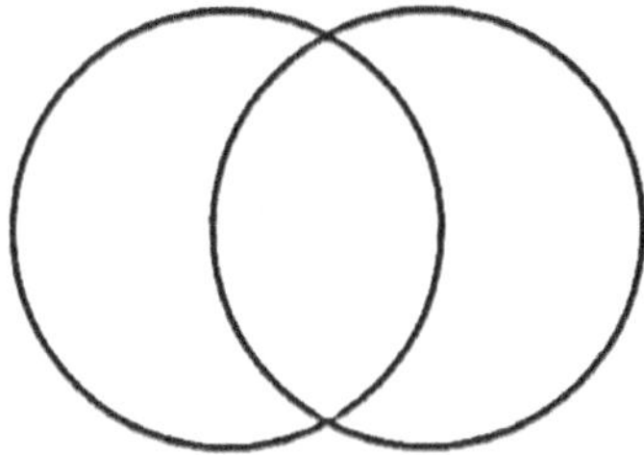

The word, vesica piscis, comes from the Latin meaning, *fish bladder*. It is a form used across cultures, and from antiquity in art and architecture. For example, the western façade of Notre Dame in Paris is the result of incorporating a descending circle that meets another circle rising from the threshold. The full vesica piscis is used symbolically as a sacred passage from the mundane outer world to the sacred inner space. Hindu, as well as Islamic holy places, have incorporated this symbol to indicate a similar sacred passage. The vesica piscis is a symbol associated with the Master Card logo which suggests that anything is possible because: in the focusing of two circles, a third energy is generated to create the Third Space. This Third Space is where all further geometric forms emerge to create a space of infinite possibilities.

> *All the effects of Nature are only the mathematical*
> *consequence of a small number of immutable laws.*
> *Pierre Simon de Laplace*

The vesica piscis is the result of focus. An example of a vesica piscis would be focusing both eyes to create a unified field of vision. A miraculous transformation of consciousness takes place with this unified field of vision.

If you were to drop two stones simultaneously into the water, the resulting series of waves would create a similar pattern and would reveal a connecting resonance, a visible energy field created by the waves' movement. On closer inspection, a perceptible line appears, connecting the two circles at their centers. Center to center, point to point, heart to heart, the interconnecting line defines the nature of the dialogue between self and Self or Self and the circumvent world; it is the heartbeat between mother and child. The line is representative of the dialogue between both hemispheres of the individual human brain. The integrity of the connection is dependent on *focus*; connection is what the lover seeks or makes the poet swoon. It is the filament that can provide the resistance to set a light bulb aglow. It is analogous to magnetic attraction. The connecting line between the two circles represents the possibility of pure creative energy. This relationship is what the artist and the mystic long for.

The center point, the heart of the circle contains the inherent genius and possibility of the individual circle; it is much like a seed. All points do not make a beautiful circle: they break down somewhere in the expansion to the periphery. Poor education, ignorance, hate, and prejudice allow discontent to direct the path from point to the periphery. Revolt, war, and chaos become means to an end where uncontrolled emotions fuel hatred and armies. War as a means of redefining any paradigm is an outdated technology. War as a means to an end is the definition of a mind that is creatively bankrupt.

There are three kinds of violence: one through our deeds, two through our works; and three through our thoughts... The root of all violence is in the world of thoughts and that is why training the mind is so important.
Eknath Easwaran.

Marginalized populations, women, and children are the ones who suffer from the failures of society. Human trafficking and prostitution become a way of life when war is the solution. Power is expressed as violence coerces, separates, and demands conformity. Power for the sake of control mystifies and is profane. Violence is emblematic of a soul sickness. It is a pathology that finds expression in bullying and gang mentality.

We actually feel the attraction as a viable force in all relationships. If you have ever spent any time on a high school campus the phenomenon is self-evident.

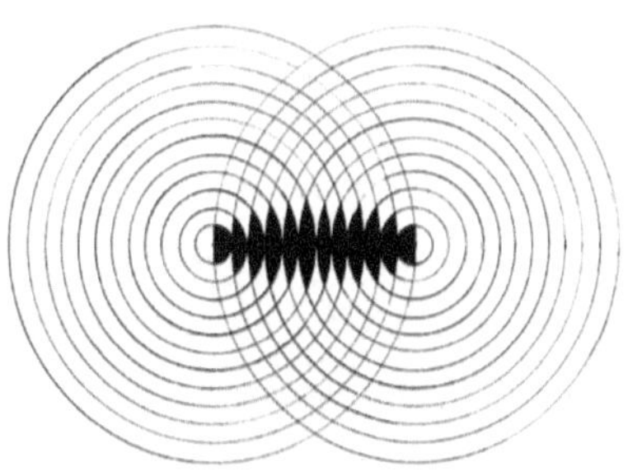

Friends, lovers, family members, and communities who make meaningful connections form simple to complex vesica piscies, I am sure that a sigh, giggle, and laugh are the sounds of this merging of shared commonality. If laughter is the sound of human connection, then a child is a genius of connection, logging in a good three hundred laughs a day. I found the following statistics on the teacher's bathroom wall at a local school here in Missouri. Children laugh 300 times a day compared to adults who may laugh only fifteen. No wonder antidepressants are prescribed *four hundred* times more today than they were in the 1980s.

> *Laughter is the shortest distance between two people.*
> *Victor Borge*

This celebration of laughter that I found on the bathroom wall continued by relating that: laughter energizes, connects us, facilitates faster learning, enables us to better retain information, and allows us to be more willing to make mistakes. What is most interesting to me was that even here in a Missouri elementary school laughter is not a secret, but underutilized. Here, I found support for the importance of engaging both sides of the brain. Here it was written that: laughter engages both the left and right hemispheres of our brain, therefore stimulating creativity and relieving boredom. Laughter builds teamwork and, innovation, and encourages divergent thinking and problem-solving. If we strive to laugh a minimum of even thirty times a day, we could change the world!

> *It takes life experience to establish oneself*
> *as a proper One.*
> *However, not all individuating processes*
> *result in a beautiful circle.*

Nature creates by shifting and confronting form; similar reactions to a laugh and giggle can be overheard. When night meets the young morning light, at the break of day, birds awaken to herald in the new day. Not just in my backyard, but all along the sun's path, around the world, we can imagine one continuous chorus celebrating a brand-new day. There is something remarkable and sacred taking place.

After months of cold, snow, ice, and fog, the Great Being Winter finally touches the sleeping heart of Spring. The first sounds here in Missouri are the little tiny frogs called peepers. Their sweet song is a much-awaited event signaling the migration of snow geese and the arrival of robins, grosbeaks, cardinals, and red-winged blackbirds. In Los Angeles, yucca pushes themselves up from the earth in a great demonstration of phallic delight, as if saying, "Hellooooo, Spring." Soon, these stalks burst into flower, as if to celebrate the coming of fairer days. The birds and insects together sound as though a party is going on along the path of spring.

Another declaration is at the close of the day, with the last vestiges of sunlight, as night begins to fall, as the first star begins to shine, the earth releases a slight sigh, a breeze comes up, and the fireflies begin to sparkle in the night. Magic.

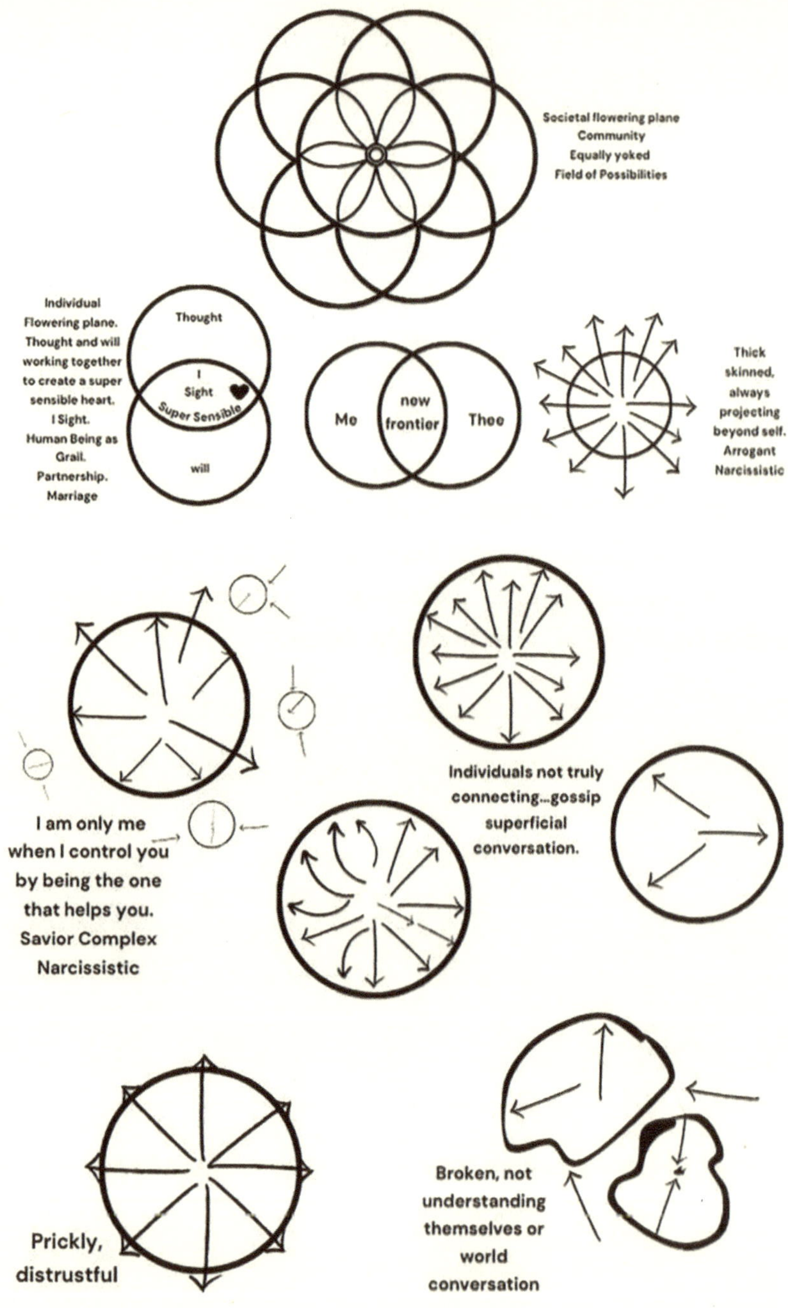
Societal flowering plane
Community
Equally yoked
Field of Possibilities
Individual Flowering plane. Thought and will working together to create a super sensible heart. I Sight. Human Being as Grail. Partnership. Marriage
Thought
I Sight
Super Sensible
will
Me
new frontier
Thee
Thick skinned, always projecting beyond self. Arrogant Narcissistic
I am only me when I control you by being the one that helps you. Savior Complex Narcissistic
Individuals not truly connecting...gossip superficial conversation.
Prickly, distrustful
Broken, not understanding themselves or world conversation

DYNAMIC EXERCISE

An interesting experiment is useful to educate a sense of interface with the world. Stand hand to hand, palms touching, with a friend as in the figure:

Now exert pressure in each of your friend's hands. Depending on your friend, you can experience a playful discourse or fall into a collapse as your friend offers no resistance. This dynamic at the periphery is very illuminating to the power of Life, engagement, and sense of Self with another human being. Leaning, and retreating… it is difficult to impossible to remain either totally passive or totally aggressive. It's the Tai jih, the yin and yang, at work.

Similarly, an encounter with the world would yield the same dynamic. The world presses in on us, and through individual technologies of prayer, art, religion, or love, we continue the self-esteem to maintain a focus or center. There are times in everyone's life when this integrity between focus and periphery can be compromised. The world trespasses on our Life and we cave in and encounter the inner beast. This is the cave of the *dragon*. Winston Churchill called his beast a black dog. Like a dog (spiritual dyslexia where life seems backward and live feels more like evil?), it can follow you around as though hunting your soul. Depression sets in. Few words can adequately describe the sense of hopelessness and feelings of alienation—it is like inhabiting an alien nation.

I was once asked to transport a couple of cows to a neighbor's new farm. My horse trailer, with a pull-down tailgate, became the cow hauler. The cows were docile, so I had no trouble leading the first one to the point of entry. She approached the ramp once, twice, three times, at least, but, bless her heart, even though she gave her best efforts, in the end, she became so overwhelmed with her lack of understanding, even with all her efforts, she could not grok how to walk up the ramp into the trailer. She met the periphery of her understanding and collapsed into a death-like faint. There she lay on the ramp, sound asleep, and no one could wake her. We tried pushing, shoving, and beating her with a stick to wake her up; we even brought out the dogs to bark at her to wake her up. Finally, with the entire racket, she managed to right herself, and we got her into the trailer. This was a startling illustration of how I have felt in the face of the unknown. I too have fallen into a collapse of consciousness and have just wanted to sleep.

COLOR EXERCISE

Another approach to shed *light* on the impact of the outer world on the inner world of our senses is to prepare a square of saturated Color—say red. Gaze upon the red for thirty seconds and then divert this gaze to a white plane. Amazingly enough, green will hover before your eyes as if in answer to the question, what is the complement of red? What makes red whole? There is a scientific explanation for this, as to how the retina absorbs light. I will offer a different explanation.

Everyone has a witness who offers commentary to questions posed to the Self. An uneducated voice can sound like monkey chatter, but with a little work, this voice can articulate amazing truths. Try this exercise with other colors to have an interesting dialogue with the unseen.

BIOFEEDBACK

In 2001, I did some work with a biofeedback technician friend of mine. I have been very interested in the quality of the interface one being has with worldly substance. He had some interesting programs that led me to believe that the *witness*, our silent partner, is always at work, making sense of whatever it is exposed to. One program was designed to facilitate relaxation. We can be either too much in the world (and then a little chilling out is essential), or too passive, and need to engage in a genuine way. In the horse world, we call "soft eyes" the ability to look without a *hard focus* that draws all your attention to a central point, but rather to have a peripheral awareness of yourself in time. The term "second attention" describes this as a meditative awareness. Finding the middle space, with the right amount of tension, is crucial. Too awake is too aware, and we know we do not want the opposite extreme of sleep. The middle realm is, of course, just right. Let's call this Lucid Dreaming. Buddha's fable of stringing the lyre gives color to this idea when he describes that a lyre string will break if strung too tight, or sound will die if left too slack. "Fair is the dancing," he says, "when the sitar is tuned."

I was directed to relax as I watched a scene of the Grand Canyon on my friend's computer screen. As I waited, not knowing what to expect, a butterfly appeared. My interest sparked, and another butterfly, and then another butterfly, and then a whole fluttering of butterflies, filled the screen. Inwardly, I felt the thrill of observing the invisible made visible. The program shut down and started again. This time, the butterflies appeared even faster. The experience was similar to the "Hundredth Monkey" concept, which states that when a certain level of understanding is achieved, awareness proliferates at an accelerated pace. It didn't take long after the program restarted for butterflies to show up immediately. An invisible Self had learned something new.

The second program was equally engaging. Without conscious effort on my part, I sat back to watch some impulse in myself make contact as a sense of the game presented itself. Now the reward was to stay relaxed, yet conscious and involved. On the screen were a pyramid and a sphere. For the longest time, nothing happened. There was nothing I could do to force change on the screen, so I sat back to listen to Jim's music and to contemplate my morning ride with my horse, Moose. Yes, I was paying attention, but was more entertained by the memory of Sacramento springtime, a willing four-legged friend, and beautiful music. I noticed movement on the screen from the corner of my eye. There was definitely movement. And then the fascination began. Fascination mixed with gratitude and what I know to be love of the moment seemed to activate the sphere. I brought a *hard focus*, and the sphere fell. Slipping back into a reverie of sorts, the sphere rose again until it could balance on the pyramid. Rising and falling, rising and falling, and then the image of the sphere rose *off the screen*. The screen became transformed by a burst of light! It was almost orgasmic! Gratitude and joyful engagement became active ingredients at this threshold of experience.

Everything in life that we really accept undergoes a change.
—Katherine Mansfield

There is the magic spot where focus changes the relationship between the observer and the observed. Take a magnifying glass to see something beyond natural sight or use a magnifying glass to focus the sun's rays. Voila—the Goldilocks Zone of just the right distance can focus the sun's rays to either send signals from afar or ignite a roaring fire. This is the original definition of Focus—hearth's fire.

MAKE YOURSELF INTERESTING

The mind doesn't wander around in sleep without a purpose.
It wants to bring back shapes and angles, Golden
Ratios, oceans and mountains—it
wants to make order out of chaos. It seems to want
to be this. It wants to dream up stories.
—Popie Mohring, master gardener

Calling on the invisible powers and making one's self more interesting to the unseen can be as simple as demanding of yourself mindfulness of the miraculous just prior to being taken over by sleep. A request can be as simple as, "May I, in the course of the day, see reflections of my striving." First thoughts and last thoughts of the day can carry a *resolve* into sleep that can impact the nature of dreaming. Alter the direction of an aimed arrow by just a degree, and its path will be considerably different one hundred yards away. Little changes make your life interesting to the creators of reality, and they make a big difference in where you arrive in the long run.

Ritual enables us to live a life
that is much closer to what our souls aspire.
—Maalidoma Patrice Somé

By 1976, my life was like a set of puzzle pieces from too many puzzles. I had not had a place to call home for my entire life. As a child, my family moved frequently. This pattern of impermanence persisted well into my adult life. At twenty-seven, I was diagnosed with a pre-cancerous cervix and then, much to my parents' dismay, I got myself pregnant. My doctors and parents agreed I should abort the child to avoid activating the cancer. I was so sick because my life had broken down. I had no higher inclinations that could keep it together. The alienation I experienced was far greater than I will go into here. I wasn't into sex, material success, or money. I didn't feel much of anything and couldn't remember the last time I'd had a good laugh. Living was a lot of trouble, so the mission I gave myself was to find some good reasons to live, or, except the repercussions.

I did not get an abortion.

I set about discarding everything in my life that was not real. I managed to fit what was left, my whole life, into a VW bug. I vowed to meditate two times a day and live according to the Ten Commandments.

My beloved Rian was born prematurely, weighing three pounds, and seven ounces. Being a single mom was so much more difficult than taking care of my dog! I regularly found myself with nothing left to give and would weep and then find amazing strength I did not know I had.

When Rian was two, we moved to an old 1950s trailer, interiorly constructed with beautiful wood paneling, and all the corners were round and soft. The simple kitchen stove required a match to light it. I had no vices, but enjoyed a cup of tea in the evening and one in the morning. The stove required a match to ignite the burner to boil water. Saturday night came around, and I found myself with one lone match. The question I was faced with was this:

Do I have a cup of tea tonight and spend the match,
or spend it for a morning cup of tea?

As I was keeping the Sabbath, I could not go out to buy matches the next day, I chose the evening tea and gladly assumed the consequences of my actions. The following morning, I was in charge of the children at church. Rian and I dressed, ate a cold breakfast, and arrived on the playground. While pushing a child on the swing, I noticed a book of matches in the sand. Finding a book of matches is in itself serendipitous, but this book's cover was blue with white writing that read:

It's been a privilege to serve you.
The back read:
Thank you, Merci, and Gracias.

The more your eyes are opened to the miraculous, the greater the realization that Grace transforms who you are. Ask for communication. The conversation will evolve over time to reflect a shift from needs and desires to the gratitude for courage and the opportunity to experience Grace and the acknowledgment of a far greater presence directing the events in your life.

I learned this, at least, by my experiment:
that if one advances confidently in the direction of your dreams and
endeavors to live the life which you have imagined,
you will meet with a success unexpected in common hours.
—Henry David Thoreau

GARAGE SALES AS A SPIRITUAL TEACHER

Garage sales may seem an unlikely stage on which to discover the mysteries of supply. As a single mother, I had to rely on something greater than myself. I became enchanted by invigorated by our Saturday bike rides across levees and down the streets of Sacramento. She rode in the child's seat behind me while, on the way home, she held the bag of treasures, our bounty from the morning adventure. Together we found everything we needed and I learned:

1. It makes a difference with whom you travel and shop. Rian and I still have a blast shopping on Saturday mornings, but not every friend believes in garage sale magic. Their disbelief makes it difficult to impossible to find the treasure. Who you hang out with makes all the difference in the world and can be the determining factor as to what treasures you find. Don't hang out with the wrong people.

> *Never spend time with people who don't respect you.*
> *—Maori proverb*

2. Every sale has something just for you even on a Sunday afternoon; it is possible to score big. So, don't get negative when the prize is hard to find. Persevere.

> *Nothing in the world can take the place of Persistence.*
> *Talent will not, nothing is more commonplace*
> *than unsuccessful men with talent.*
> *Genius will not; unrewarded genius is almost a*
> *proverb. Education alone will not;*
> *the world is full of educated derelicts.*
> *Persistence and Determination alone are omnipotent.*
> *—Calvin Coolidge*

3. Never settle for less than you want. Never take something home that requires fixing. This includes men! If found broken, you can find it whole. Set your expectations and anticipations high, and don't settle for less.

Cost is what you pay; value is what you get.
—Adapted from Warren Buffett

4. If the price is too high, it isn't yours. I never offer a ridiculously low amount, as I am willing to pay what I think an object is worth, and I do not think it is ideal to try to get by as cheaply as possible. Poverty consciousness is tacky. If I really want something, I still offer what I am willing to pay and accept that something else will manifest. It is entirely within the Garage Sale Manifesto to find a similar item at a better price. Don't pay too much, and if you are the one selling, never, never give it away.

Value is determined by the buyer
Worth is determined by the seller.
—Warren Buffett

Know your worth.

5. Lastly, it sometimes takes a bit of time to warm up to the process. Not to worry. The key is to stay engaged and interested. This pertains to meditation well as to garage sales, cross training, and horse training. There needs to be a commitment of effort to secure results. A twenty-minute commitment is often what it takes to find the zone whether it is a second attention, congruent relationship with your horse, or the second wind a runner gets.

The same energy that moves
thoughts through the mind moves the stars across the sky.
—Stephen Levine

EXERCISES

Rudolf Steiner suggests six basic exercises for spiritual development. The following are three of the exercises that are designed to strengthen and focus the three primary human qualities: thinking, feeling, and willing. Though seemingly simple, these exercises work on the portals of personal perception to bring about harmony and integration in the soul's life.

1. One of the indicators of intelligence can be to evaluate how long a person finds a simple thing interesting. The first task is to take a paper clip, spoon, or pencil—the simpler the object, the better. Clear your mind of everything else but the object.

   The goal for ten minutes is to either hold the image of the item in your mind in all its detail or think only thoughts pertaining to the object. For instance, thoughts might include: how it was made, where it was made, who made it, and the materials that went into its making.

   Simple things can take on an amazing complexity to become intriguingly interesting. Directing one's attention for an extended period of time helps to heal lives too heavily influenced by technology. Do this every day for a week.

We are being transformed,
even at this very moment,
by our extraordinary velocity
and the emergence of a newly insistent force
—the power of now.
—Stephen Levine

2. Assuming we have elevated thoughts doesn't assure immediate effective living. Broken wills are easy to find. Environmental crisis overwhelms the heart, and war threatens to polarize our nation to eliminate what innocence is left. There is so much happening all around us that can break the will.

    This exercise seems deceivingly simple. Decide on an act to be performed daily at a specific time. Twist a ring or stomp your foot at a specific time. The deed should not carry with it any consequence or personal meaning. Do this for one week. One day is easy, but to persist requires mindfulness and the ability to allow your thinking to penetrate into the deep recesses of your will.

3. Apparently easier still is the exercise for the heart. The only instruction is for you to give up annoyance, disappointment, frustration, exuberant happiness, and sadness. In this exercise, one aspires to autonomy, equanimity, and equilibrium. Only a stilled heart is able to see the subtle difference in appearance. Emotion is a byproduct of experience. Feeling, on the other hand, perceives qualities of the observed. Sympathy and antipathy are polarizing emotions that separate the observer from a true experience of the perceived. *I like it* or *I don't like it* reveal more about the observer than the observed.

    The results of this exercise are obvious. Try sitting by a forest pond. At first, the landscape may appear as though no one or nothing lives there. After sitting quietly for a while, the pond reveals its secret Life as ducks emerge, fish rise to the surface, and birds begin to sing. Silence can call forth a multitude of experiences.

    These three exercises strengthen the soul to help it avoid collapsing in the moment and to stay in the Now. Anger, loss of center, arrogance, or embarrassment disrupt soul currents and cause a collapse of consciousness. I wonder what deep sorrow caused a Southern belle to take to her bed for days. Could the vapors have been such a collapse?

HOW TWO BECOME THREE, OR THREE BECOME ONE

We who aspire to fulfill our earthly mandate are "charged" to become more fully human. Often this journey is launched out of pain, heartache, or a longing to know what lies behind the veil of the physical world. We develop an authenticity, or spiritual focus, in much the same way as a child creates a unified visual focus. Tinkering around with basic premises, bringing into focus I and Thee, me and the other (or rest of the world), we create I sight. I sight is essential to navigate the supersensible middle kingdom created by I and Thou. Both eye sight and I sight are created by the Light.

> *I know, of course, that trees and plants have*
> *roots, stems, bark, branches, and foliage that*
> *reaches up towards the light.*
> *But I was coming to realize that*
> *the real magician*
> *was light itself.*
> *-Edward Steichen*

Focus is the key, but not a given. It is essential if one is to redefine "limitation" presented as the earthly curriculum. *Focus*, imagination, and courage catalyze a new beginning, where a new *I Am* establishes a singular awareness. You have to be the spiritual optometrist who can focus the image of the world onto the supersensible heart to obtain *I sight.*

Love is what focuses the heart when it is faced with the realization that everything else as other. It is the natural evolutionary sequence to confront the dualistic nature of physical existence to bring about a qualitative change. How this paradox is reconciled requires artistry; especially today when populations have become so polarized on even the simplest of issues. It seems like overnight we are a nation divided.

News Release: The latest poll indicates 49 percent are for the latest issue and 47 percent oppose it. Four percent have no opinion. I wonder about those people who have no opinion! What are they thinking? What we think and what we do become so polarized that our lives are torn apart, making us vulnerable to pundits, politicians, commercials, and the notion that war is the answer to making the world safe for the United States. This is very unimaginative thinking! It is a malady of the soul that even clutches at the hearts of our children. We are a society that thinks one thing and does another, or, worse yet, acts and does not know why. Democrats blame Republicans and vice versa. Aren't we all Americans?

NATURAL INTELLIGENCE

Looking to the natural world, we may observe that Nature is faced with the dualistic conundrum as well. Nature is not either/ or, either. Where there are extremes, a living reconciliation occurs. Here, on the periphery, there is Life. A new approach, a new gesture, a new expression is created. Perception is not solely what we see, but as Nature informs us, also what can be imagined.

All Nature points to a greater whole that when perceived
magnifies the meaning of the individual parts.
Goethe

Sacred Geometry names the Third Space, a mandorla, or the vesica piscis. I call it a Sacred Door that leads to a creative sphere virtuously untapped by humans. The Third Space or Sacred Door is created by the yoking of thought and deed. The vesica piscis of our being is the supersensible heart created between you and the rest of creation. Uniting what we think and do creates a heart, a heart thinking, whose beat is the background music to a Life in progress.

But, there is more. Every time an apparent limitation is redefined, a new potential heart begins to beat.

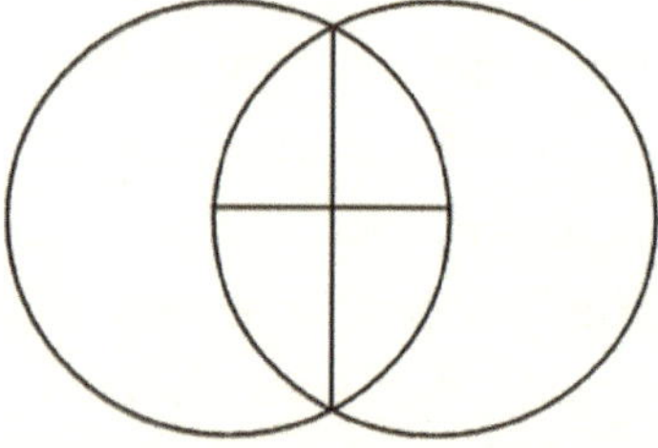

The reconciliation of opposites, the resolving of paradox, creates a cross within the vesica piscis. The primary geometrical form created by connecting the apex and center of the vesica piscis is a cross.

The cross is who you really are and is the I Am. The cross is created as an individual learns to stand on his or her own two feet; the cross is formed by standing straight, on your own two feet, and reaching out your arms. *"Take up your cross and follow me* asks that a person reconcile for themselves the apparent duality; to come to terms with the apparent polarity to form individual perspective based on Love. This yoking of apparent separateness, of reconciling opposites is not a new idea. The New Testament offers that this is the *I Am."*

My yoke is easy and my burden is Light.
—Matthew 11:30

Light, as in the ability to see, carries with it a responsibility when you can see where to go and what to do. As the creative potential within stirs, basic loving mindfulness is essential. But creative potential must be nurtured and fed if one is to embrace all life experiences to bring about living truths that go beyond the superficial. The burden of Light can also ask, what we do now that we know. For every step we take in understanding, we need to take two steps in the application of that understanding.

All too often, learning and growing becomes one-sided, distorted, and myopic, lacking the creative dynamic necessary to flower into the full potential of an individual capable of acting in Freedom. What passes as Freedom is hardly free. Freedom is a worthy contemplation because if you ask ten people what is the definition of Freedom, you will no doubt get ten different answers. To be Free requires a more thoughtful response than is normally given. Without getting into long philosophical treatises on Freedom, I would like to offer that Freedom comes from a refined sense of Self that can act and respond to a situation without preconception, sympathy, or antipathy, but with the perception *to know* the situation. How we choose to think about the world, ourselves, and Nature is a matter of choice. Thinking can be educated to ever finer perceptions.

> *But yield who will to their separation,*
> *my object in living is to unite*
> *my avocation and my vocation,*
> *as my two eyes make one in sight.*
> *Only where love and need are one,*
> *and work is play for mortal stakes,*
> *is the deed ever really done*
> *for Heaven and the future's sakes.*
> *—Robert Frost,*
> *"Two Tramps in the Mud"*

CHAPTER 5

The Shift as Flowering Plane

*The body must be nourished, physically, emotionally
and spiritually. We are spiritually starved in this
culture—not underfed, but undernourished.*
—Carol Horning

The word religion has become a general heading into which all interpretations of a higher power have been filed. The many expressions of reverence point to what His Holiness the Dalai Lama teaches in that each path to enlightenment is unique; ideally, there should be as many religions in the world as there are people.

There is no need for temples,
No need for complicated philosophies,
My brain and my heart are my temples;
My philosophy is kindness.
—-Dalai Lama

This notion, however, is hardly encouraged. Threats of excommunication, being burned at the stake, shunned, or eternally damned have kept the doors to salvation closely guarded; with a fall into a fiery pit. The Inquisition and the book burnings of Savonarola, and even the extreme ascetics who confronted the Buddha on his way to enlightenment, coerced the naïve into believing that the individual has little to contribute to his or her own salvation, and that denial and self-abuse would unlock the doors to Paradise.

He who possesses art and science has religion.
He who has neither had better have religion.
— Goethe

The seeker of the Truth and not the shadow of the Truth must be vigilant at all times, lest she collapse in fear, sadness, or horror at the possibility that the heart of the mystery not be revealed. Jesus was crucified because he preached that everyone could cultivate a deep, meaningful, personal, and interactive relationship with the Almighty. It is, in fact, the Father's good pleasure to give us the Kingdom. Our desires are known before we speak them; we are loved beyond a shadow of a doubt. This is the Christian teaching; so fair warning to all of us, the path leads us right through the forces of Death and Resurrection. Saint Paul suggests we should learn to die daily. Practice makes perfect. I have learned that by allowing little deaths to my personal preferences on a daily basis, I am not so surprised when bigger challenges come along. I am quicker to realize that I have collapsed in a death-like faint, and therefore, quicker to return to Life. Maybe,

The best mind-altering drug is Truth.
—Lily Tomlin

For many, the American Dream is a belief in the material promise of abundance for everyone. The promise of freedom and the pursuit of happiness has come to mean: A chicken in every pot and a car in every driveway. However, the United States was founded on the principles of a spiritual freedom that has demonstrated the possibility of a far greater freedom. Many of the original settlers to the New World came here to escape religious persecution. Freedom and pursuit of happiness meant a fulfillment of dreams for self-expression. The Declaration of Independence from King Charles was the first of its kind to separate a people from a supreme authority. It set a people on the path of what George Washington called the Great Experiment. The question then and now is whether or not human beings have the maturity to govern, first themselves and then create a government free of corruption. Our Founding Fathers recognized the weakness of character that could undermine the realization of human evolution. To this end, the United States has spawned many profound thinkers; our history has exposed the greatest threat to human dignity in its battle against slavery. The enslaving of not only a human being, but also the human heart has proven the necessity of constant vigilance. Thinkers like Ralph Waldo Emerson and Henry Thoreau and people of conscience like Thomas Jefferson, George Washington, Ben Franklin, FDR, JFK, Maya Angelou, Annie Bessant, Ernest Holmes, Napoleon Hill, Eleanor Roosevelt, Joseph Campbell, Bill Moyers, Juliet Gordon Lowe, Alan Ginsberg, Martin Luther King Jr., Joseph Smith, Joseph Smith, Susan B. Anthony, Elizabeth Caddy Stanton, Mary Baker Eddy, Amy Goodman, and my great Aunt Maggie, who served her love of humanity in the baladi (slums) of Cairo, these people have made our country great. Americans have been instrumental in the worldwide defense of human rights. We have gotten dolphins out of tuna, and protested to halt the Vietnam conflict. In 2011 a twenty-four-year-old woman started a petition that caused Bank of America to back down from initiating fees on individual bank transactions. The results are not yet in as to what the lasting effects of the Occupy Movement will be, but one thing is clear. The American people enjoy freedom, not only because of our armed forces, but also because we have been raised up by the good people of our country, who have fought passionately to overcome the perceived evils of their time. Freedom is not the justification to do just as we please, but it offers the possibility to redefine life experience in accordance with ideals that inform our thinking.

If I have seen further, it is by standing on the shoulders of giants.
—Attributed to Sir Isaac Newton

To this end, the etymology for the word religion comes from Latin, meaning respect for what is sacred. Wikipedia details the origin of the word religion as obscure, but might be traced to Cicero connecting *lego* (to read) and *re* (again). Joseph Campbell's definition comes from a form of *ligare* (to bind, connect) with the prefix *re* (reconnect). Certainly, religion is a verb that offers practical steps to know a personal god, and sets the soul on the path to cloister or practice.

> *Freedom is born out of a capacity to work with*
> *any energy or difficulty that arises.*
> *—Jack Kornfield*

The medieval alchemists portrayed themselves as blind men following in the footsteps of Natura, the highest expression of Nature. They believed that Natura, or Nature, had the ability to teach the secrets of Life, enabling them to transform the common earthly experience into the gold of spiritual insight. Contrary to Emmanuel Kant, whose thinking has deeply influenced Western thought, Goethe believed that human thinking could bridge the gap between the natural world and the human soul by developing intuitive intelligence. His worldview challenges the observer to come to his or her own judgments based on imagination and keen observations of the natural world. The intuitive capacity unites sensory impressions to bring meaning to the natural world. The activity is very much like the uniting of words to make a sentence. As we know, the ability to perceive the parts cannot produce content; only the imagination can imbue content with meaning. Content is the result of understanding the relationship between the parts and the whole and is arrived at through the activity of sacred individuality. There are people who justify their hatred and anger because they live in a world that does not make sense. How we bring meaning to our sensory experience ultimately determines the quality of our understanding and whatever peace is in the world.

The power of imagination makes us infinite.
—John Muir

Goethe believed it possible to perceive the secrets of Nature through observation and the cultivation of imagination. Like any created object, the thoughts that went into creating it are there for the practiced observer. Likewise, Goethe believed it possible to know the thoughts—the elemental Life that created the clouds, the trees, animals, and flowers—by understanding the language of metamorphosis and change. He believed science and art come from the "primal source of all being," and because we, too, come from this source, by knowing Nature we can know the author and ourselves as well. Nature gives riddles. She never completes a picture, but demands the creative thinker to struggle toward a revelation. The struggle to find the resolution creates organs of perception in the soul.

Intuition is a spiritual faculty and does not
explain, but simply points the way.
—Scott Shinn

Plants and human beings are yoked in a reciprocal relationship that makes us mutually dependent. We are like a precious stone placed in an emerald setting. Without plants, our planet would not be able to sustain Life. We are dependent on plants for food, oxygen, healing, and mediating the potentially destructive rays of the sun. By day, we breathe in the oxygen and breathe out the carbon dioxide that the plant breathes in. Conversely, at night, the process is reversed. This reciprocal relationship creates an expansion and contraction, a greater breathing between two kingdoms, as though together we make one being. The laws of Nature work for us, not against us to become a more refined and artistically productive creation.

Like us, the plant connects heaven and earth. Intricate root systems under the influence of gravity grow down into the darkness while the lighter forces of levity lift and fashion plant substance. Their life cycle is played out balancing forces of levity and gravity, sympathy and antipathy, contracting and expanding—growing from point to periphery. In the plant, we can witness elemental forces of earth, fire, water, and air at work, and we can study the language of gesture through the laws of Nature.

> *The creation of 1,000 forests is in one acorn.*
> *Ralph Waldo Emerson*

Through a series of contractions and expansions, a plant rhythmically grows toward fulfilling its genetic code. The meristem cells, or the undifferentiated plant cells at the growing point, function much like human stem cells. These cells provide the genius of differentiating—creating leaf, stem leaf, and the possibility of a flower. Goethe's observation led him to connect petals to leaves as a metamorphosis of form. The flower is the result of a problem-solving strategy in the plant itself. The flower is a gift to the sun and the result of redefining limitation at its best. Further refinements are fragrance and pollen that enable the plant to attract another hierarchy and to reach beyond itself … clever little buggers.

> *From top to bottom, a plant is all leaf, united so inseparably*
> *with the future bud that one cannot begin to imagine otherwise.*
> *—Goethe*

The plant world offers a wealth of contemplative material for the seeker of self-knowledge, as the plant's evolution parallels our own struggle to become more of who we are in an ever- expanding desire to know what we are made of. It is by desire that all things blossom. Each plant has a story, as it is a living analogy for problem-solving strategies that have developed countless species over thousands of years. Each story is about the plant's dilemma to know and reach for the Light. Goethe's imagination of the plant was that there is an archetypal, supersensible plant that the plant yearns to manifest. In the evolutionary sequence of things, the plant struggled, adapted, changed, and created reproductive organs in the form of a flower.

The plant evolved over millennia from undifferentiated algae in the great waters of the world, where it metamorphosed bladders to raise itself out of the water, into the Light, and onto dry ground. Through a process of differentiation that refined the plant's process through the spore and gymnosperm, the plant reached the periphery of its ability; the plant reached its *flowering plane.* The leaf made an evolutionary leap to flower. The flowering plants evolved much later into what could be considered the gift to the Light, created by the intense yearning to become more, a perfect manifestation of *plant.*

> *Come bright butterfly close to me,*
> *your beautiful wings are so nice to see.*
> *You fly like a bird, you sip like a bee,*
> *but you're really a flower the wind swept free.*
> *—Novalis*

Goethe observed that change does not happen in a linear fashion, but rather evolves to a point of limitation. At this point of limitation, the plant has to find a new problem-solving strategy to continue to develop beyond its genetic code. The place where the plant reorganizes into a flower is called a *flowering plane.* How a plant organizes itself and at what level of *becoming* it has reached tells us a great deal of what lies behind the particular plant.

The struggles a plant goes through to make itself more perfect are distilled in essential oils and flower essences. These healing substances can be used to work gently over time to realign the intentions of a person's striving. In the distilled plant essence or oil, is in fact the result of a plant's genius transformation toward flowering. The rose, at its peak of perfection, is quite possibly the most differentiated flower to be formed at the periphery. Further evolution could only be simplified, as in the case of the lily. Here, its parts have become so streamlined in its venture to the Light that it looks as if the sun has drawn it up in one loving swoop. The lily is so refined that it has become the symbol of ultimate purity and forgiveness. Each species of plant is a process, a snapshot in time of the plant's becoming. Hidden in its proportions are the archetype and gesture of the plant.

> *Little flower—but I could understand what you are,*
> *root and all, and all and all,*
> *I should know what God and (wo)man is.*
> *—Alfred, Lord Tennyson*

Flowering trees are excellent examples to ponder as to how a particular tree meets its periphery. Some plants meet their limitation joyfully. The tips of their branches grow upward, and at the point where they can go no farther, a flower bursts forth. The magnolia, gardenia, and crepe myrtle, to name a few flowering trees, are perfect demonstrations of this hypothesis. The weeping willow, on the other hand, does not seem to experience its limitations or boundaries in the same way. It grows endlessly, without flowering.

The bud stands for all things,
even those things that don't flower,
for everything flowers from within,
of self blessing; though sometimes
it is necessary to reteach a thing its loveliness,
to put a hand on the brow of the flower, or retell it in words
and in touch, it is lovely until it flowers again
from within of self blessing.
—Galway Kinnell, poet, Mortal Acts, Mortal Words

Could the human being be the result of creation's yearning? If so, Christ is the archetype that the soul desires to embrace. Christ revealed all that is humanly possible in responding to the universe, the One Call to Life to flower to grow beyond our natural tendency to remain the same. The flower of a plant and the human being entered the archaeological record about the same time. The flower is to the plant as the human being is to creation. Creation has become conscious of itself in the human being. The world is a reflection of the Many in One, and the human being is the result of the One in the Many.

We can easily forgive a child who is afraid of the dark,
the real tragedy of life is when adults are afraid of the Light.
—Plato

What calls the sunflower or the palm tree to grow to great height while remaining balanced and grounded, defying gravity, yet tethered to the earth? Mystics of old, Plato and Aristotle, tell us of the music of the spheres—the sound of Creation becoming. The subtlest expression of the Divine calls to us in each of our dreams to become more. It is *beauty* we long to embrace. Who doesn't want to love with abandonment, or to follow the siren's song into the unknown?

To work magic is to weave the unseen forces into form,
to soar beyond sight,
to explore the uncharted dream realm of hidden reality.
—Starhawk

The human being unites the worlds of Light and Darkness through creative activity. Plants and humans both flower in the presence of Light. As the physical eye is created by the Light, a corresponding I is fashioned by an inner Light. The iris, a flower of sorts, surrounding the pupil (student), allows Light to reveal the world. The function of darkness and Darkness is to open the pupil to the Light. I speculate that when up and down, right and wrong, Light and Darkness, male and female, wolf and lamb come together in reconciliation, a Sacred Door will swing open, and the music of the spheres will spill out of heaven. This will be no common music with audible notes, but the sound of Silence—the music between the notes will precipitate like morning dew on the soul.

The notes I handle no better than many pianists.
But the pauses between the notes—ah, that is where the art resides.
—Artur Schnabel

And the day came when the risk it took to remain tight in the bud was more
painful than the risk it took to blossom.
—Anaïs Nin

After silence, that which comes nearest to expressing the inexpressible is music.
Aldous Huxley

What would you do for Love? The rose returns from the collapse of winter with an amazing determination to bloom again. Even the violet, as shy as she is, is one of the first ones back after winter's snow. How did these delicate creations of Nature achieve such subtle refinements and have the courage not to collapse in fear or be too overwhelmed to bloom? Similarly, how do we find the courage to Focus our Light into the darkness of the unknown and ignite a fire and bloom?

How did the rose ever open its heart and give to this world
all its beauty? It felt the encouragement of light against
its Being; otherwise we all remain too frightened.
—Hafiz, Sufi Master

Humanity is quickly approaching a threshold, a flowering plane, a Shift. Depending on who or what informs your thinking, this can be a great adventure or a terrifying meeting with the sins and omissions of a life not lived. There are forces that limit perception and fragment understanding. The closer to this *threshold* we get, the more we experience a dissonance, which appears in the relationships of all things to all things. Unsurprisingly, the medical field has a pill for this malady that affects us all, and even our children. As a culture we no longer value core ideals of beauty, reverence, and awe. The public educational system has failed to prepare our children for a world that pulls the heart in every direction. What happens when constructive life patterns fail? Evolution is achieved only in the binding back of opposing forces into a central focus.

Let knowledge grow from more to more,
but more of reverence in us dwell:
That mind and soul, according well,
may make one music as before.
—Alfred, Lord Tennyson

The goal is not to escape matter, as in the Eastern traditions, but to acquire dexterity of spirit to move through an encounter with the natural world. The human being evolves as potential capacities, previously uneducated, begin to function at the periphery of experience in a creative, imaginative, questioning, and listening manner. My prayer is:

Teach me to hear mermaids singing, to hear the harmony
of the spheres, to be Bathsheba's David, and
to follow my muse into myself.

It is up to the individual to cultivate imagination of transformation as a prerequisite for spiritual activity. Facts alone will not bridge the worlds, heal the spirit, or harmonize the soul. Creative thinking is not bound in the head.

Rudolf Steiner, in *Knowledge of Higher Worlds and How to Attain Them*, pointed to latent spiritual power that flowers in human consciousness because of individual effort. East Indian mystics also call these spiritual centers *flowers or chakras*. Since the Renaissance, humanity has flowered in its individuality, but it now faces an evolutionary conundrum.

Seataka is the term in Yaqui meaning personal medicine, or personal power. This power is considered a great gift we are given at birth. Literally, Seataka means "flower body," suggestive of a kind of power, although Yaqui people hold that the English word, "power," is inadequate. The Yaqui believe that individuals are born with specialized gifts. Seataka, the most important of these gifts, is said to be fundamental to Yaqui thought and life. Seataka is the channel between human beings and the rest of nature.
—Dictionary of Native American Mythology

Through a study of art history, we can visually follow the evolution of consciousness to this threshold. Creative intelligence is always in process and always searching for an evolutionary path.

Historically, evolutionary consciousness has experienced a series of evolutionary collapses and transformations that have demanded a reorganizing and restructuring of creative energies that interact with the natural world. By looking at art history in this way, we can see art as the articulation of human consciousness as it meets worldly experience; perception is much more than what the eye sees. Art is the visual content of an age, culture, or individual Life. Art is then the picture of how consciousness and creativity meet the periphery. Here at the borderlands is a threshold, where Life is happening and where all the action is taking place. Art is the outward expression of these impulses coming in contact with the inner life of mood, inspiration, and sensation.

Art then becomes a verb describing a form of perception, a part of the human psyche that seeks out the unknown on the borderland of consciousness, where the willing may encounter a new world through refined perception. Like the plants, we have emerged from a collective organized mind to an ever more individual and complex expression of the Self.

The ancient Egyptians were guided by a profoundly initiated priesthood. The monolithic statues of motionless pharaohs upon their thrones still convey a quality of destiny. Rudolf Steiner spoke about how such individuals still had the ability to sense the workings of the stars and cosmos in their bodies. To achieve this connection to the stars the pharaohs had to achieve an absolute stillness. Even so, with this gesture of stillness, one can perceive a future calling to become someone on one's own. Art describes this activity of the sacred individuality grasping its purpose to become more self-aware. Art is the creativity in the individual to discover within itself refined statements of Self. What refines the plant to flower, is present in the individual as Art. It is active ingredient in the refining of individual to bloom in the inner Light.

Art is a form of the verb to be.

Is this just an interesting turn of phrase, or is there value in asking *what* does the creating? *Who* is composing? What, in the collection of human expressions, sculpts, sings, dances, or writes eloquent prose or verse? Furthermore, by expressing one's Self in such a way, is that Self more artistically intelligent? Thinking can be transformed beyond normal, mundane activity of head/brain-bound thought to be active in the will as *imagination*, in the mind as *intuition*, and in the heart as inspiration. Cognition, or awareness, is amplified and applied as dynamic at the periphery as a super problem-solving strategy. The brain feels, the heart thinks, and the will is educated and given a voice. The bad news is that you cannot buy imagination in a book or swallow a little intuition to help your day go a little better. Artistic activity can discipline and educate life forces in the realm of the sacred. Through art, every sense can be educated and raised to a higher octave of perception—to become a form of the verb "to be," as in:

How Great Thou Art.

Artistic practice magnifies what is essentially human; creativity is a purely human activity. By practicing art, one can embrace the genius latent in the soul that organizes perception and imagination. Art is the language of the soul that resides in the realm of mood, inspiration, and sensation; movement, music, color, and substance lie silent in a world not expressed. Children are natural artists. They live in this mood of soul where life is revealed in the language of symbol and picture. Indigenous people still retain this mythic consciousness in that many still remain connected to a world of myth, tone and color; they retain an intimate connection to Nature and still think in pictures.

We in the horse world have witnessed how the intelligence of a horse has been radically redefined as horse lovers have learned to communicate in more horse-appropriate ways. This acceleration of perceived intelligence has occurred not because horses were getting smarter on their own, or because of horse people like Monty Roberts, Pat Parelli, or Buck Brannaman, but also because women have had a voice in the field of horse training. Many of us believe this acceleration is because we experience that horses can see our mental pictures. This is a modality that lies close to the human soul and the exercise of it in partnership with one of these beautiful creatures is satisfying beyond belief. Horsemanship is therefore as much about training the person as it is about training a horse. That being said, a horse is still limited by its DNA and genetic code. A horse will not take on a project of its own volition. A racehorse can be trained to perform to excellence, giving itself beyond a once-perceived ability, but to date, records are set and occasionally reset within only microseconds. Human beings, however, continue to crash through ceilings of performance and redefine what is possible in every sector as we learn to dream bigger and better—sometimes just for the fun of it.

Dreams unfold in pictures, and pictures create meaningful content within which fine details and invisible processes can be studied. This is storytelling at its very best. Learning to think with pictures is learning to think holistically, imparting on the student a unique capacity to learn from the environment and raise experience to a kind of poetry.

> *Poets are the unacknowledged legislators of the world.*
> *—Percy Shelley (1792–1822)*

> *Too many people in the modern*
> *world view poetry as a luxury,*
> *not a necessity like petrol.*
> *But to me it is the oil of life.*
> *—Sir John Betjemen*

Pictures defy judgments based in sympathy or antipathy, so the student must learn to hold the mind steady to allow the picture to surface and then have the moral capacity to explore the visualization. Pictures easily vanish from view; they flee a cold stare and must be coaxed to remain in all their vividness.

If your everyday life seems poor, don't blame it; blame yourself; admit to yourself that you are not enough of a poet to call forth its riches; because for the creator, there is no poverty and no poor indifferent place.
—*Rainer Maria Rilke*

I deeply remember my struggle to be understood. My perception was an amalgam of feelings and ideas that appeared like a mirage to my mind's eye. Few people had the interest or inclination to try to understand what was arising and disappearing in my experience. This was my fulcrum of evolution, as I moved from the world of images into coherent thought. I desperately wanted to be real.

The journey between what you once were and who you are now becoming is where the dance of life really takes place.
—*Barbara DeAngeles, author of Passion*

The Mermaid's Tale is the story of this journey into the meaningful and how Life's initiations have transformed my soul- life to be compatible with my worldview. In the pursuit of the beautiful, art has been the transformative agent and has brought me to question what forming concepts and receiving impressions and sensations have in common. I know *thinking* does not take place in the head but is liberated from words and intellectual constructs to be synthetic and engaged by poetry, painting, movement—the arts. Through the arts, I have experienced a sort of digestive process of personal, creative intelligence searching for meaning, somewhat akin to photosynthesis, that quickens my heart as it participates in the unfolding of destiny.

> *We are shaped and fashioned by whatever we love.*
> —*Chuang Tzu*

Healing the senses is only a part of the greater work, but in the process, the senses weave together a subtle body that can perceive finer realities. Anthroposophy, the body of work of Rudolf Steiner, focuses on the development of the lower senses that metamorphose into ever-finer preceptors of experience. Feeling and sensation are everything. They are not the collecting and assembling of characteristics but are a living process that allows imaginations to surface and pictures to form. Young children observe with their whole being—they don't separate themselves from the notion of good or bad, or *I like* or *I don't like*. They recall details that, as adults, go unnoticed.

Observing over time, we can experience dynamic cycles of transformation or enigmas of the human personality that cannot be measured or quantified. The living world is imbued with qualities that interact with substance. Warmth is more than a temperature. Warmth softens and blends; it releases fragrance and sensation; it transforms and changes water or cooks food. Warmth has the ability to purify. We can experience the quality of warmth in relationships to personality traits; and in the extreme love, but also anger.

If we could but step back a bit from our process of seeing the world, we might come to the conclusion that there is a substantial amount of information bombarding our senses that we simply do not process. Clearly, city life provides so much stimulation that shutting down is a matter of self-preservation. We take in information rather passively, sensing the outer world through the lower five senses of seeing, hearing, touching, smelling, and tasting. There is however an inner world of sensing that begins to mature as we take part in the mystery of Life and relationship. The senses that inform us of our inner experience are the senses directed inwardly. Thought arises from sensory impressions that form basic images. We have an outer experience and an inner one as well.

The sense of well-being is most likely overlooked unless we do not feel well. It takes in a wide spectrum of sensations that include not only a sense of Life, but also movement and balance.

Touch is more than the experience of rough, smooth, bumpy, or slick. Touch encompasses all the senses because through them we not only touch the world, but it touches us. Through the sense of touch, we touch all of Life, and in so doing, we experience ourselves. It encompasses the haziest, dreamiest touching to the most noble of all, the touch of being "in touch" with other people.

The senses give pleasure and they can also stimulate thought. Just as we can train our senses to register nuances of timbre, clarity, and melody, our senses can also register the higher constructions of melody, or that the sounds that form words have a meaning. Hearing can be the foundation for the perception of speech and more refined still, the sense of thought.

The sense of another person is certainly a sensation that can go beyond mere sympathy and antipathy. Your family dog may be a better judge of character than what we mere humans are capable of discerning. Horses, too, behave in accordance with their reactions to each other and to people. Indigenous people once had an intuitive sense of other tribal members in order to keep the tribe coherent and safe. Most of this subtlety has been lost but can be found once again.

What we have are the senses that inform us of our own organism. Touch, Life or Well-being, Movement, and Balance.

Senses inform us of the outer world, such as the sense of smell, and taste. No arch in the sky, no green in the dew, no color on the grass, no sweetness in sugar, no fragrance in the rose, and no sound in the bell, but only phenomena taking place in external objects that have the power to cause those sensations in a living being.

Thoughts direct energy and energy follows thought. The basis of Freedom resides in having thoughts that can perceive the Truth and act accordingly. If the capacity for inner vision is suppressed, we will never have enough interest in the world or each other to go beyond appearances to bring order and beauty to a chaotic inner life.

And if not now, when?
—The Talmud

Creative energies manifest in a variety of ways. The human being is a micro-cosmos. We have a whole cosmology imprinted in our DNA, and we have ever more subtle connections interfacing with the world. Artistic activity educates these connections to integrate Self and sense, creating individual identity.

Sculpture is the most material, most dense, artistic expression. Whether chiseling stone or modeling clay, the artist's creative energy is educated to understand how form and density can be fashioned. Painting invites consciousness to participate in the subtle interplay of Color and tone. Color is the language of the soul, and watercolor the perfect carrier to instruct the soul through this refined medium. Music educates the invisible forces that lie below the threshold of consciousness and so close to the human soul that it is the last bit of humanity to be destroyed as a result of error or damage.

Everything in our world has a sine-wave signature. According to Hindu wisdom, everything emits a sound according to how it is put together. The average of all sounds is equal to 7.23 cm = *OM*: the sound of the universe humming.

All creation responds to music. Mathematics is the basic component of the universe expressed as music. Artistically, we would aspire to refine our senses to perceive the movement behind the physical and understand music in its denser form; we can learn to perceive the invisible by loving the visible. Tuning the soul to the beautiful is in itself transformative. Any of the arts not only fashions but rarifies the soul into a healing substance, as music educates the invisible forces. Perception is not just what the eye sees. The notes and spaces between them can draw us closer and closer to what creates form in the first place, and then the arts give outward expression to what comes from within. This matters more than recording what has already been—as in rendering a still life that is logical, organized, and abstract.

Sensation is everything. When the artist follows sensation rather than going right for the form, she can grasp an understanding of how form comes into being. Herein is the question of whether creativity is viewed as a means toward Freedom from all restraint or as a means of becoming free, but within limitations. Through practice, art catalyzes a force of evolution by connecting thought to execution.

Today, like any other day, we wake up empty and frightened.
Don't open the door to the study and begin reading.
Take down a musical instrument. Let the beauty we love be what we
do. There are 1,000 ways to kneel and kiss the earth.
Rumi

Impressions become feelings, and feelings create motivations. Emotions must be the individual experience based on how well the impression has been understood. In my experience, an emotion contains an electrical charge that can affect how well a thought creates awareness. An undisciplined thought life can turn destructive, while equanimity allows feeling to arise from the inner life as a moral force. It is an individual responsibility to refine sensibilities and thoughts in order to get over the confusion by which we think the fact is real and imagination an illusion.

A (wo)man should hear a little music, read a little poetry, and see a fine picture every day of (her) life, in order that worldly cares may not obliterate the sense of the beautiful which God has implanted in the human soul.
— Goethe

Clearly, the Renaissance was a milestone in outer perspective. What the soul is seeking to understand today is an inner perspective based on individual creativity. Scientists are discovering that the raw substance of the human soul can be modeled, spaced, colored, and enhanced. Thought is the active ingredient of intelligence. There seems to be unlimited potential.

It always signifies a distinct decadence in art when its mission is sought in mere amusement.
—Rudolf Steiner

Art need not be for the sake of making objects, but can cultivate the feeling life of the individual, and, to this end, to develop *art* as a teacher of the formative forces active within the disciplines of the media. Artistic activity allows for fluidity between thought and action, and in the process brings consciousness to the subtle field of individual perception.

Creativity is the natural order of life. Life is energy, pure creative energy.
—Julia Cameron the Artist's Way

Aside from the obvious development of sensitivity to observation, tuning of fine motor coordination, and engaging the aesthetic senses in discrimination, art can therapeutically assist the would-be artist in expression of thoughts and feelings that do not have words. The preordained nature of the movements to specific tasks resonates in the inner life as the practitioner adheres to defined laws inherent in the quality of the material and purpose of the object. Creative impulses within specific modalities might include balance, an inner sense for of movement, beauty, warmth, and a sense of the methodical and repetitive qualities found in Nature. Problems become opportunities to persevere in the face of the unknown in the quest for beauty, truth, and balance. A problem-solving strategy of perceived limitation engages creative life forces in an activity that challenges the life force to become more refined. The process and medium, when approached in a meditative manner, are forgiving. Error is redefined; materials like water, clay, wood, and beeswax inform the latent soul about the descent into substance. By learning to create through different mediums, we enter a world of great mystery in which the secrets of becoming are met. Order may be found where it had previously eluded awareness. Lack of understanding may be the result of a need to refine one's capacity of perception. By becoming aware of subtle nuances, the powers of discernment perceive the seen rather than one's individual likes and dislikes. What I like or do not like tells me about myself. Acceptance and interest allow the other to reveal itself to overcome spiritual dyslexia, and then, gratefully, a new world of perception unfolds. I can love, not because of personal gratification, but because I appreciate the world I find in the other.

Love is the spirit
that motivates the artist's journey.
The love may be sublime, raw, obsessive, passionate,
awful, or thrilling, but whatever it's quality,
it's a powerful motive in the artist's life.
—Eric Maisel

The ancient Greeks believed the various arts were guided by goddesses called "Muses." They were Graces to which many aspired. A Muse would guide a seeker into ever more refined perceptions. Through movement, one could refine a sense of equilibrium; sculpture, a sense of life; architecture, the sense of touch; painting, the sense of sight or Light; music, the sense of hearing tone; poetry, the sense of hearing speech. The human being in dialogue with the Muse grows into a work of art.

To practice an art is to explore the act of creation as a spiritual practice,
as a way of awakening to our true nature
and contacting the beauty and mystery of our lives.
—Ann Cashman, 1991 Yoga Journal

It is a well-accepted thought that the arts have the possibility to harmonize and enhance both hemispheres of the brain through physical and creative movement. By connecting both hemispheres and thought and deed, a would-be artist can introduce a higher expression of activity that creates a morphogenetic field in the pineal and pituitary glands of the midbrain. Hindu texts claim that as a result of spiritual practice and deep meditation, the pituitary gland excretes a spiritual substance called Amrit. One drop of this substance is thought to bestow eternal life. Having never tasted the substance, I can only dream it is a royal jelly prepared by the Self for our own evolution.

What is passion? It is surely the becoming of a person.
John Boorman

However, healthy development is more of an anomaly in today's world, as the relationship with the natural world is broken down by increased alienation. Speed and technological advances have robbed us of appropriate moral as well as physical movement. Morality in this text does not refer to a sense of right or wrong. Right or wrong are purely cultural designations. By moral activity, I mean thoughts, actions, and deeds that have conscious intention. Morality refers to the level of care directed toward a meaningful consequence. The moral of a story ascribes meaning to an action or behavior that dictates an outcome. Amoral activity is lacking in care.

To affect the quality of the day, that is the highest of arts.
—Henry David Thoreau

Apathy is perhaps the wellspring of evil. As long as one is emotionally connected to an outcome, unseen forces can direct one's glance. The future of earth's evolution is directly linked to human morality based on inner convictions in how limitation is overcome. Thought and morality have formative forces inherent in their ability to affect change. Morality is the fashioner of the heart.

Self-respect is the root of discipline.
The sense of dignity grows with the ability to say No to oneself.
—Morris Mandel

Too many children are prescribed drugs to counter social and learning disabilities without a deeper understanding of the underlying causes. Many of these disabilities can be traced to arrested development caused by a lack of involvement in the immediacy and intimacy that Life provides in a learning process. Children have their education served to them in pre-packaged facts. Self-discovery is seldom seen as a process the child is capable of, and, as a result, feeling and enchantment are educated right out of their hearts. Without direct experience of the physical world, senses atrophy and perception is minimized.

Because there is a lack of movement and dexterous expression, a fragmentation of experience creates no morphogenetic field in the brain or centers of social development at all. Touching the world and touching each other is minimized, and isolation sets in as a pathological phenomenon. Without a moral education that provides a physical or feeling movement, the higher cognitive capacities withdraw from the muscles, which become frozen or even enter a state of shock. Public education fails to acknowledge the importance of movement and involvement in simple crafts and art that engage the child in age- appropriate stages of development.

> *We must accept that this creative pulse within us is*
> *God's creative pulse itself.*
> *—Joseph Chilton Pearce*

For the span of modern research, science has held the conception that our health and fate were preprogrammed in our genes and that much of life experience is preordained. Cellular biologists have now redefined the extreme importance of the environment, the external universe, and our perception of the environment as to how they directly control the activity of our genes and DNA. There is quantum physics behind these mechanisms that provides insight into the communication channels that link the mind-body duality. An awareness of how vibration signatures and resonance impact molecular communication constitutes a master key that unlocks a mechanism by which our thoughts, attitudes, and beliefs create the conditions of our body and the external world. This knowledge can be employed to actively redefine our physical and emotional well-being (Bruce Lipton, 2000).

Candace Pert, author of the 1999 book, *Molecules of Emotion*, through a long and eventful career, came to the conclusion based on her scientific study that health and disease are not dependent on genetics and DNA. She declares that maximizing one's capacity for self-expression and increasing responsibility for one's health and lifestyle can directly affect disease prevention and even destiny.

Our environment, according to Pert, is becoming acutely polluted with chemicals and heavy metals that severely interrupt and alter electron flow, causing energy starvation to nerve centers. She states that 80 percent of all diseases are caused by stress and false perceptions that we are separate and isolated from Nature. The body then becomes a battle zone of the emotions against the body. Emotions exist in the body, while the existence of feelings, inspiration, and love appear to transcend the physical. Feelings connectors are empathy, compassion, sorrow, and joy. Fear is the biggest deterrent to understanding.

Dr. Pert's work has redefined the brain as our primary intelligence or seat of consciousness, a premise that ancient Egyptians already knew thousands of years ago. She has documented that there is a chemical flow that arises simultaneously in different systems—immune, nervous, endocrine, and gastrointestinal. These form vast superhighways of internal information exchanged at the molecular level. Intelligence permeates the entire body; it is not a hierarchical system from the head down.

The threshold is not without, but within. The new awareness must be cultivated as a newly focused heart evolution, where the heart thinks and the authentic Self speaks. We can redefine the world starting with the notion that *victim* no longer has any validity. Just as we have experienced that duality is a phantom of sight, so it is also an illusion of thought.

If a healthy human nature were to work as a whole,
if human beings were to feel the world as a
great, beautiful, and worthy whole,
if their harmonious comfort were a cause of pure and free delight to them,
then the universe, if it could feel itself,
would shout for joy at having reached its goal
and would revere the pinnacle of its own being and becoming.
—Goethe

A thing of beauty is a joy forever.
—John Keats

Beauty is truth, truth beauty....
that is all ye know on earth
And all ye need to know.
—John Keats

Art is constitutive—the artist determines beauty. He does not take it over.
—Goethe

Beauty is life wherever life unveils its holy face.
But you are life and you are the veil.
Beauty is eternity gazing at itself in a mirror.
But you are eternity and you are the mirror.
—Kahil Gibran

Beauty itself is but the sensible image of the infinite.
—Sir Francis Bacon

When I am working on a problem I never think about beauty.
I think only how to solve the problem. But when I've finished,
if the solution is not beautiful I know it is wrong.
—Buckminister Fuller

Though we travel the world over to find the beautiful,
we must carry it with us or we find it not.
—Ralph Waldo Emerson

You agree, I'm sure you agree, that beauty is the only thing worth living for.
—Agatha Christie

Beauty is an ecstasy; it is as simple as hunger.
—W. Somerset Maugham

CHAPTER 6

The Scent of the Rose

Beauty is one of the rare things that
does not lead to doubt of God.
—Jean Anouilh

Through the ages, beauty has inspired the artist, the scientist, and the lover to become more worthy of its honored presence. Beauty may be in the eye of the beholder, but there does appear to be an intangible quality of beauty that goes beyond the subjective. In the presence of true beauty, we are in awe of Nature or taken to our knees by an unexplainable presence in our lives.

I ride in the Ozark Hill country, where hills and ravines create a unique ecosystem defined by pasture, forest, and stream. Lime Kiln trail is a forty-minute ride that takes me through some of the most beautiful nature I have ever experienced. It isn't spectacular compared to the Grand Canyon or Yosemite, but there is a simple sweetness to how it is protected from the wind and cold in winter, and from the extremes of summer. The elements are in balance and content. Flowers and butterflies flourish through three seasons of the year, and, as the Japanese say, flower in snow during the winter.

What delights us in the visible is the invisible.
—Marie Ebner-Eschenbach

It is not what we look at, but what we see that is important. Reverence for beauty cuts across all cultures. The key to all beauty is in the simplest of expressions found in proportions, or ratio of how the parts relate to the whole.

Pythagoras, or at least one of his pupils, is credited with the discovery of the Golden Mean or Golden Ratio. The Golden Ratio reveals the mathematical matrix behind manifested form; it is a signature that incorporates the limitation as a determiner of transformation and growth across all kingdoms. What we find in Nature is likewise represented in the human form.

The Golden Mean resonates with personal meaning, as the refined definition applies to symmetrical proportion, free of dissonance or genetic flaws. It appears to be the happy medium between the two extremes of excess and deficiency. There is a single organizing principle behind creation. The first Law of the Universe is Order—it is for you, not against you.

Beauty, as well as compassion, and forgiveness, exists outside of time. These virtues are portrayed in Greek mythology as inspiring the neophyte to love beyond her imagination of self and safety. Depending on whom you read, the Muses sprang from the movement of water, and the striking of air, were only embodied in the human voice, or arose from three chords of the ancient lyre. Another account tells how Pegasus, the white- winged horse, struck the ground with his hoof, causing the spring of Helicon to gush forth. Here in the sacred well, nine nymphs became the Muses. Athena, the goddess of Love, tamed Pegasus and presented the mighty horse to the Muses. They are responsible for the source of all knowledge, visual art, theater, dance, literature, and poetry. And then there are the Three Graces who embody grace, beauty, joy, charm, and virtue. They are everything in the world that anyone could wish for.

By the Middle Ages, the Muses and Graces were revered in the worship of Mother Mary. The Holy Mother inspired the troubadour who sang praises of courtly love. No poet could grow conscious of the Muse except through a woman in whom the goddess was to some degree a resident.

> *Bait, n: A preparation that makes the hook more*
> *palatable. The best kind is beauty.*
> —*Ambrose Bierce*

Beauty inspires but also ensnares. The shadow of beauty is so hypnotically seductive that it can cause the unprepared to collapse into faint-heartedness. Western traditions do not prepare us for the transformational consequences of this kind of falling in love. Hindu philosophy honors Kali; Greek mythology has stories of Hecate; and the story of Briar Rose has the Thirteenth Wise Woman.

BRIAR ROSE

Once upon a time, there was a king and queen who said everyday "Ah, if we only had a child." But they never got one. One day as the queen was bathing in the dark waters of the unknown; a frog (a symbol of metamorphosis) crept onto dry land and said, "Your longing shall be fulfilled, for you shall realize the magic of your own becoming." In due time, their heart's desire came to pass. The Queen brought forth a lovely daughter. The king was so overcome with the beauty of his creation, that he ordered a great feast to which he invited not only his friends and relatives but also the Wise Women of the land so that they might be kind and well-disposed toward the child. There were thirteen Wise Women. However, the king only had twelve golden plates for them to eat off of, so one had to remain at home and uninvited. This decision not to invite a Wise Woman because he did not have enough plates to go around appears fairly arbitrary, but then again, it points to a limitation stemming from the perception of limitation of the King.

Thirteen marks a transition: There are thirteen cards in a suit, and thirteen keys in the chromatic scale from C to C- eight white keys and five black. Thirteen guns in a gun salute, thirteen steps to the gallows, and thirteen in a baker's dozen. Julius Caesar crossed the Rubicon with the thirteenth legion. Jesus plus his disciples made thirteen. The Torah mentions thirteen Attributes of Mercy. A child of the Jewish faith matures at thirteen and any child becomes a teenager! The number thirteen has a curious and much-maligned reputation in the West. Thirteen is what defines this tale, and is therefore significant to the Wise Women, who were not witches, but women. The fact that there were twelve and that the thirteenth goes unrecognized points to something much deeper. The Feminine has long been rewarded for its beauty but overlooked for her role as a co-creator in the great mystery of Life. What is uninvited to the celebration turns out to be as significant, if not more so, than all the beautiful gifts. There must be a secret to the overlooked and invisible. Even though the archetypal Feminine has a passive countenance, look below the surface to an activity that is determined to be recognized at all costs.

Hindu mythology does not limit the Feminine to only lady-like virtues. The Feminine has many faces, but Kali, the dark Mother of Creation is also the consort to Shiva, the prime mover of all the worlds.

Black mother goddess, salt dragon of chaos, Sebuoulesa, Mawu, attend me, hold me in your muscular arms, protect me from throwing myself away.
—Audre Lorde, African American poet

Kali has multiple manifestations, ranging from the goddess of Time and Change, to Redeemer of the universe. She creates and she destroys. Her name alludes to the qualities of Darkness, Time, and

Death. All creation arises from her, like bubbles from the sea. It is in the confronting of her that assimilates and transforms her into a vehicle of salvation. She may be linked to the destructive elements, but also to the creative. Sometimes thought of as destructive and dark, she is also the ultimate reality. Through her, one rids oneself of fear.

Hecate is a Greek goddess of crossroads and entrances. She wields womanly power because she is connected with witchcraft and the moon. Though not as fearsome as Kali, she is the guardian of thresholds who watches over doorways, gates, walls, and childbirth. Surely, her presence is needed in times of delicate transitions, where protection can make the difference of destination, intrusion, or life and death. These active ingredients of the Feminine soul-life go unheeded. Nobody wants to hear that change is upon us. My guess is that this is not the first or last time the thirteenth Wise Woman wasn't invited to the party.

The adversity the kingdom encountered was a threshold of sorts, wherein the culture underwent a Shift. The perceived evil was the element of limitation imposed on the kingdom in order for a new life to invigorate the land. Change must happen. As we have seen, it is a law of the land. Even if we are not a part of the process, we are not excluded from the ramifications of a universe in progress. Unless we are conscious participants, we, too, will fall asleep along with the flies on the wall.

There are many interesting uses of the number thirteen in history that can lead us to believe the number points to an opportunity for something not understood, but vital to survival, to be introduced into the story. We are in awe of this mighty number, enough to rename a floor with its number or to be extra careful on a Friday the thirteenth. The Kabala has thirteen circles on the Tree of Life, so something mythical must be possible with its manifestation.

Western patriarchal culture honors the solar calendar with twelve solar months. The Asian calendar, on the other hand, is derived from the thirteen lunar months. In this tale, we hear how difficult it is to bring the two hemispheres - the Western king - Eastern queen- together for a new order or kingdom to survive.

The hidden wisdom could be instrumental to the salvation of the United States, in that there were thirteen original colonies, there are thirteen horizontal stripes on the flag, and the Great Seal of the United States has thirteen olive branches, thirteen olives, and thirteen arrows in the eagle's grip. Thirteen characters make up *E Pluribus Unum* and *Annuit Coeptis*. It is no secret that the soul of this country is in jeopardy. The natural evolution of democracy finds its greatest expression in the spiritual values that the nation embraced to overcome tyranny and the limitations this tyranny imposed. Its fall comes to pass in the loss of the passion it took to gain its freedom.

To return to Briar Rose, the king's feast was celebrated with all manner of splendor, and when it came to an end, the Wise Women came forward to bestow their magical gifts upon the child. One gave virtue, another beauty, and third riches, and so on with everything in the world that one can wish for.

When eleven of them had made their promises, the thirteenth Wise Woman came forth, wishing to avenge herself for not being invited to the feast. Without recognizing any guest, she approached the cradle, and in a loud voice proclaimed: *Before she can realize her significance to creation, she will die...all of the kingdom will wither with her death. When she is fifteen, and before she reaches the age of her majority, a spindle will pierce her heart, a shadow will cloud the kingdom, and all that is innocent will perish.*

The hall fell silent in shock and horror, but the twelfth Wise Woman, whose magical gift remained unspoken, came forward. Although she could not undo the evil wish, she could soften it. She said: "Not death, Oh daughter of a king, but slumber as my gift I bring. One hundred years your needs must sleep with roses red the watch to keep."

ADVERSITY

Now, the king could hardly bear that what was so precious to him would ever encounter anything but the ideal of perfection. Daughters, especially pretty ones, are often idealized and therefore shielded from the consequences of being human. The princess remains in a dream state.

He believed that he had the power to avert what had been decreed, and so declared that all spindles be burned to ashes. Every father and mother wishes their child was born with a manual to coach her through those first few, formative years of life. We stand in awe, as we witness the emerging personality assert itself to master her body and environment. If at all possible, wouldn't we shield our beloved from every bump in the road or every limitation that might cause discomfort? Try as we might, there seems to be an unseen hand at work, pulling the strings of destiny. We administer vaccines to thwart illness, and, heaven forbid that a child be ill with a fever. Most children have some device that eliminates true mastery of learning to walk. Well- meaning parents prop up the little tyke in a seat with wheels and somehow, as if by magic, the child is propelled across the floor and around the house. Where is the taste of victory for a battle fought and won? Don't struggle too hard, and don't go near the water. When we miss crucial stages of development, we may not be prepared for the test that is big enough to cause real damage.

Viruses mutate and bones break to teach creative intelligence how to triumph in the face of hardship.

Waking from the sleep that birth interrupts is slow, and bringing order to a body takes artistry. The whole child is a sensing organ that learns by ascribing meaning to what can appear as an arbitrary world. In this dream, the world touches the feeling life of the dreamer to guide her descent into the waking world. Every obstacle informs the emerging scientist of how and what it is to confront the unknown: she can either transform it or be transformed by it. Learning takes place at an exponential pace until around the change of teeth when the round, chubby, child transforms into a slender student of Life. Ideally, the child is allowed to dream her way into the world. Playfully, thought is cultivated into the possibility of complex strategies.

If the king is the archetype for intellectual thought, the lack of the ability to think for oneself is the stumbling block to salvation. In this story, it becomes the princess's undoing.

> *We are most deeply asleep at the switch*
> *when we fancy we control any switches at all.*
> *—Annie Dillard*

Meanwhile, the gifts of the Wise Women were bestowed upon the child, for she grew so beautiful, modest, good-natured, and wise that everyone who saw her was bound to love her.

No matter how much the king wanted to spare the child, he grew complacent and soon forgot the secret force of prophecy at work in his kingdom. Oh! How quickly we forget! On the very day the prophecy was to be fulfilled, he was nowhere to be seen and his beloved daughter was quite alone to wander about creation to see what lay behind every door, just as she pleased.

The consequence of allowing the young to wander around creation, just as they please, is all too obvious today. Drugs, unwanted pregnancy, and rioting in the streets are products of the young who grow up unprepared to encounter real life.

Where ritual is absent, the young ones are restless or violent.
—Malidoma Patrice Somét

It took no time at all, less time than could be imagined, for the princess to find a staircase that led to a door that conveniently had a rusty key in the lock.

A rusty key can only mean that the door opens to an ancient wisdom. The staircase leading to a tower is the higher mind that, unless well- educated, becomes destructive. Education should be directed at guiding this incredible force to maturity, but tragically these forces are never dormant. The Western culture of physical beauty and personality ushers in a pseudo-maturity that can wound the emerging soul. This is when the Little Mermaid met the old crone, the Goose Girl's false identity, and Briar Rose her antagonist.

Even though the decree was not a secret, no one really knew how it would come to pass. The stage was set well in advance, and all the princess had to do was walk through the door.

Her curiosity so overwhelmed her that she knew not what she did. She turned the key and the door swung open effortlessly. Even though there were windows all around, they were shrouded, and an old woman sat in the middle of the room spinning, softly speaking to herself. The child felt compelled to listen to the drone of the crone (who could have been Kali herself) and her spinning wheel, who told her: *You have no control over the events of your life. What you see is all there is…Happiness is an illusion. You will die and all you have done will be in vain. Your happiness is of little consequence, and your only truth is in self-sacrifice.* Unable to understand, the princess moved closer as the old woman continued to tell her of disease and poverty that afflicted those outside the palace walls.

For the first time in her life, the princess's eyes were opened to the sorrows in life and she felt a pain pierce her heart and became overwhelmed with her own inadequacy. Paralyzed by fear, she could not run away but collapsed into a death-like faint.

Spinning is an archetypal image used to symbolize thinking. If it is refined enough it can link together thoughts that penetrate the nature of the world. This higher thinking is permeated with potential. What the princess heard and what was said could be two separate things. The thirteenth Wise Woman could have also said: "Life unfolds before you. You have two choices; one to embrace life, and the other to withhold of yourself. The sorrow therein comes to all; the rich and poor, righteous and unrighteous. But, have faith, for there are great mysteries to be revealed to you if you do not fall asleep or collapse in the face of adversity. Life is not about accruing worldly possessions or just being happy and comfortable. If you don't try to evade the life you have been given, there will be help for you all the days of your life. Everything works for the powers of the Almighty."

The art of spinning is to create from beginning to end, without breaking, one continuous thread. The significance of the deeper symbolic meaning would be to stay alert while linking together impressions into thoughts and then concepts at least one not follow a "thread of thought" to its rightful conclusion. Perhaps there is nothing more common than superficial thought that prematurely appears as Truth.

Such it is that a limitation be placed upon the growing princess who, without the intrusion of limitation, may have grown to be beautiful, but not a vital influence in the kingdom. Not death, but death's little sister is the chrysalis into which the budding personality slept. Sleep is the destination into which we escape—a protected realm of archetypes and dreams where new meaning can be ascribed to riddles of existence.

A dream that is not understood is like a letter that is not opened.
—The Talmud

At this juncture into adolescence, many young girls seek a resolution to the baffling changes taking place in their bodies. Hormones propel the seeking heart to find love somewhere. Without appropriate direction, one could be misled to believe that quest is outside her. Lacking direction, the heart collapses into a mere shell of itself. There is a mystery to the Goldilocks Zone of being not too awake, but not too asleep; it is a middle realm where Lucid Dreaming reveals the synchronicity of events. This princess reached out to the wrong person. Unfortunately, it is experience that teaches us that it makes a difference in what we think, and who we hang out with.

The old woman smiled as sleep descended upon the castle and further out into the kingdom. Even the king and queen, who had returned too late, fell into a deep sleep. All came under the enchantment of nothingness—even the flies upon the wall. The breeze ceased to move the leaves on the trees, and a great shadow fell upon the land. Fear spread far and wide, cursing the land with drought, pestilence, war, and famine. Cows no longer gave milk, children could not be comforted, and music was heard nowhere. Thorns grew where once beautiful fields prospered. For you see, there was no king or queen on the throne. Even a hive of bees knows that royalty is the unifying force. Within a short time of its queen's absence, the hive will show signs of collapse. And so it came to pass that the kingdom slept on unaware because no one was awake at the switch.

Time passed—harder for some than others. Soon obscured, the castle all but disappeared from view. All the while, a thorny hedge of mistrust, greed, and superstition grew about the castle walls, so all that could be seen was the golden spire that shone like a flaming sword in every direction to announce the way to the castle.

A warrior must take care that his spirit is never broken.
—Chozan Shissai, Japanese swordsman

And so the story of the beautiful, sleeping Briar Rose, or so the princess was named, went far and wide. Many came to hack their way through the thorny hedge to take the kingdom by storm with the power of conviction and mantra, but they had no love in their hearts and so were caught fast by the thorns, and they and their dreams died a pitiful death.

Thankfully, hope did not die, for a champion had been born. Some called him Parzival, but though royal blue blood ran in his veins, he had red blood, just like you and me. The *great forgetting* had not touched his innocent heart, and so the desire to know his humanity still burned.

Dissuaded as he might have been by those who had tried and failed before him, he guarded his thoughts and steeled his heart to advance in the direction of his longing. Long years of caring for the land and ministering to his subjects had cultivated in him compassion and a willful determination. He believed that death was an illusion, that resurrection was as real as the flowers that bloomed every spring, and that every battle was one waged against himself. As he advanced toward what for some meant certain death, the hedge began to bloom with roses, butterflies flew forth, and the hedge parted of its own accord.

We have met the enemy and he is us.
—Pogo (Walt Kelly)

There is one thing stronger than all the armies in the world,
and that is an idea whose time has come.
—Victor Hugo

We are raised and enhanced by the efforts of the few. In good times, those honest efforts come to fruition, and like the hundredth monkey, everyone benefits as a tipping point is reached.

Taking your journey requires you to leave
behind the illusion of your insignificance.
—Carol Pearson, The Lesson

THE ROSE

Michael S. Schneider, in his 1999 book, *'Beginner's Guide'*, leads us through the imaginations behind the differentiation of form as experienced through Sacred Geometry. We have already witnessed the creation of focus and the illusion of duality that forges the vesica piscis, or Third Space. In so doing, the vesica piscis is really a functional three-in- one and one-in-three. The primary forms that emerge through the vesica piscis are the straight line, cross, triangle, square, and cube; all can be easily drawn using basic tools of the geometer. With some imagination, one can perceive this metamorphosis as the evolution of the plant from seed (point), stem (straight line), leaf (plane), and form (volume).

*The bud stands for all things, even for those things that don't
flower, for everything flowers from within itself of blessing;
Though sometimes it is necessary to reteach a thing its loveliness, to
put a hand on the brow of the flower, and retell it in words and in
touch, it is lovely until it flowers again from within, of self blessing.*
Galway Kinnell

Five is the number of petals of the rose, and the rose is a representative of five as an archetype. The rose is the example of the most differentiated flower in the plant kingdom. Five is also symbolized as a star or the pentagram. Throughout antiquity, the method of constructing a pentagram was kept secret and selectively passed by word of mouth. The method was published in 1509, when Fra Luca Pacioli, Leonard da Vinci's teacher of mathematics, revealed its geometric construction. This construction was considered magical, as the construction of the star requires complex execution. The knowledge of which became a sort of insider's code of recognition. The pentagram, like the starfish, has the inherent properties to regenerate itself indefinitely. The first insert on page XIII and the following insert illustrate the dynamic power of the Pentagon to regenerate itself.

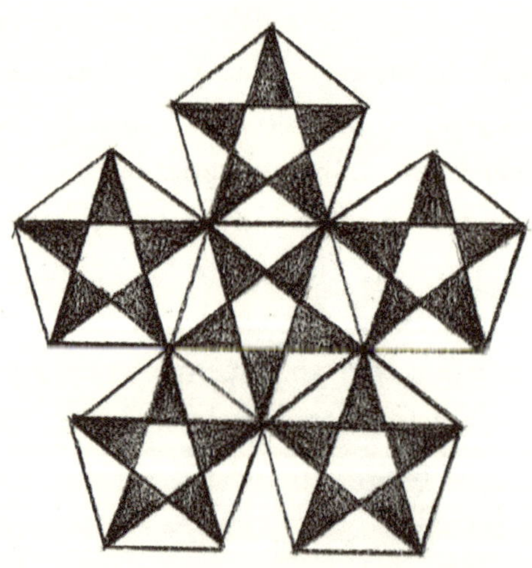

Five is seen throughout the natural world as the archetype behind leaves, flowers, starfish, and the center seeds of an apple. All these symbols offer the promise of regeneration. The archetype of five contains the mystery of Nature by expressing the magical proportions of spirals, the Fibonacci series, and most extraordinarily, the Golden Mean. Schneider takes the reader through the experience of the various constructions. The experience is so gratifying that I recommend that curious readers take the mystical journey through his book.

For our purposes here, the five-pointed star is more than a symbol of the highest performance of beauty and efficiency. It also defines the human body in its highest expression and refinement. We are stardust and we appear to be a star when we stand with arms extended and feet outstretched. In number five, the star reaches its refinement of beauty, form, and energy; the flower achieves refinement in pollen and scent and is transformed into an elixir that tempts the next hierarchy to pollinate it so that it may attain new life. Five marks a departure into the possibility of a living world. The full journey to ten requires yet another book.

AWAKENING

The prince walked through the hedge, into the courtyard, and all was so still that not even a breath could be heard. Nothing was as he had feared. He wandered around until he too found the spiral staircase, and opened the door to find the sleeping princess, his slumbering soul mate. She was all that gave reason to live— all that could create beauty, and Beauty itself. Briar Rose was all that had been promised.

He bent down to kiss her cheek, and in that very moment a bell could be heard tolling in the distance; light filled the chamber, and all the land was bathed in a rosy glow of holy anointing. Flowers bloomed everywhere, a breeze came up, and the rains came down. Birds sang, and the king and queen awoke from their enchantment. And the prince and princess grew to reign over the kingdom in peace.

> *All beauty is making One of opposites,*
> *And the making One of opposites is what we*
> *are going after in ourselves.*
> *—Eli Siegel*

CHAPTER 7

Phantasies

"I have never concealed the fact that
I regarded MacDonald as my master,
indeed I fancy I have never written a book
in which I did not quote from him."
C.S. Lewis

The last story comes from George MacDonald. He wrote for children as well as adults who he takes on a journey through our dreams and imaginations. His writing is the rarefied writing of fairy tales themselves. The following is a fine thread he wove through Phantastes; the story of Anados's awakening.

A young man, by the name Anados, received a key for his twenty-first birthday that gave him access to fairyland where he could wander at will. His encounters with women defined his journey as he pursued some and was hunted by others. After many of these encounters, he heard music that drew him into a clearing in the forest. There sat a young woman tossing a golden ball on high. As the ball left her hands, it quivered like quicksilver and hummed like a harmonic sphere. She was so entranced by her plaything that she didn't notice his approach. And he became so enchanted by the maiden's beauty and her shimmering golden orb that he lost all sense of propriety; he reached out to touch the ball. Horror of horrors, the ball shattered into thousands of pieces. All that was left was a puff of black smoke.

"You broke my golden ball!" she wailed. She ran into the forest and no matter how he pleaded, it was of no avail—she disappeared and we do not hear from her again until the end of the story.

He blundered around fairyland learning from some, but ignoring others to his peril. It was, in fact, such a time that he ignored the advice of one of the fairyland's caretakers. "Do not open the door at the rear of your chamber!" he was warned. After a brief battle with his inclinations, he opened the door and watched, to his bitter amazement, a shadow form emerge from the darkness and attach itself to his heel.

The shadow proves to be a depressing travel companion. He found that at every happiness, the shadow moved to disenchant a child's toy, the love of a friend, and every shred of joy or hope he held as Truth. This shadow was the unredeemed in his life that had been allowed to come to pass because he had not refined his perceptions. His senses betrayed him by not informing him of the true nature of the phenomena he encountered. He perceived outer beauty, and in an attempt to possess it, his curiosity took him beyond his ability to sustain alertness.

After trial and inquiry, he found himself in the ruins of an old castle; he became a prisoner of his own concepts and construction. By day, he was held behind the thick stone walls, while by night he was able to wander in the illusion of freedom. Each night his hope was renewed, but when the sun rose, he found that he had not been released from his torturous predicament. While lamenting that yet again he found himself a prisoner, he heard from outside his prison walls, the joyous sound of a woman singing.

The sun, like a golden knot on high,
gathers the glories of the sky,
and binds them into a shining tent,
roofing the world with the firmament.
And through the pavilion, the rich winds blow,
and the birds for joy, and the trees for prayer,
bowing their heads in the sunny air,
and for thoughts, the gently talking springs,
that come from the center with secret things—
all make a music, gentle and strong,
bound by the heart into one sweet song.
And amidst them all, the Mother Earth
sits with the children of her birth,
She tendeth them all, as a mother hen,
her little ones round her, twelve or ten:
oft she sitteth, with hands on knee,
idles with love for her family.
Go forth to her from the dark and the dust
and weep beside her, if weep thou must,
if she may not hold thee to her breast,
like a weary infant, that cries for rest,
at least she will press thee to her knee,
and tell a low, sweet tale to thee,
till the hue to thy cheek,
and the light to thine eye, strength to thy limbs,
and courage high
to thy fainting heart, return again,
and away to work thou goest again,
From the narrow desert, O man of pride,
come into the house, so high and wide.

He was so moved by the grace of her song that he easily found the door that had eluded him throughout his captivity. How shocked he was when he could easily escape his prison. Restored to freedom, he approached his liberator, "Thank you, thank you," he cried, "Were it not for your song, I would have never found my way."

She answered, *"Do you not know me? You broke my golden ball. Yet I thank you. I do not need the ball any longer, for now, I can sing. I could not sing before and now I go about singing till my heart might break for the very joy of my own songs. And, wherever I go my songs do good, and deliver people. And now I have delivered to you and now I am so happy. Had you not broken my golden ball, I would have never learned to sing."*

This is a beautiful moment in which purpose can be ascribed to the tribulations we so carefully try to avoid. In an effort to avoid pain at all costs, we can miss experiences that transform the soul and mature the person. She, the liberator, was once liberated herself from the enchantment of external gratification. Mesmerized by what glitters and shines, she was actually inhibited from refining her artistic talents. Lack of forgiveness would have held her captive, but once there was no hopes of retreating to the past, she turned her attention to find an inner beauty. We are so easily mesmerized by appearances of beauty that one seldom asks what lies within. The slumbering soul will continue to dream if not properly educated. Art and thinking are one single organizing principle that can take the dreamer from seductive, coy, and scheming to self-initiated individuality.

The self-same well from which
our laughter rises was often times
filled with our tears.
The deeper that sorrow carries into our being,
the more joy it can contain.
—Kahil Gibran

Only after he has been held captive and come to terms that he was what he was and no *longer sought to behold if not his ideal in himself,* at least himself in his ideal could he, too, find forgiveness. Through trial and test, he recognized a secret pleasure in judging himself as inadequate. In his new light of day, he rested in the simplicity of being no knight, and not his shadow, just himself. A new resolve entered his heart as the old shadow passed away. He looked for it but did not find it. Our traveler encountered a threshold of personal involvement when he acknowledged in himself the disparaging shadow thought life and the liberating experience of forgiveness.

Last night as I was sleeping I dreamt—marvelous error that I had a beehive here inside my heart. And the golden bees were making white comb and sweet honey from all my old failures.
—Antonio Machado, poet

There is nothing like a trip through fairyland to disorient the senses and confound the soul in its quest to synthesize direction and meaning from an alien landscape. We, too, tend to wander about in life until we learn a few basic lessons that put who we are into a righteous perspective. Not knowing is all right. Organs of perception can be created by a willingness not to know all the answers.

Be patient toward all that is unresolved in your heart and try to love the questions themselves.
—Rainer Maria Rilke

Leonardo da Vinci, an archetype of human creativity himself, called this attitude of soul *fumato.* He considered it a necessary attitude of soul in order to be actively creative. *Fumato* is a state *of radical unknowing* in which the questions are more important than the answers. *Fumato,* or radical unknowing, allows Life to be a paradox. The would-be artist cultivates the ability to live with ambiguity and uncertainty. The process of allowing is what we sometimes experience as suffering. By surrendering to the events as they come to meet us, capacities in the soul come to Life. The process becomes the product, where a creative tension stops chaotic worldly impressions, so that revelation can rise from what, in effect, we already know. Creativity does not depend on some imagined innocence. We are already good enough.

> *To become aware of the subtlety of*
> *Nature, you need to be alert.*
> *The moment you become alert, you*
> *become still…thinking subsides.*
> *That is actually a higher state of*
> *consciousness than thinking.*
> *—Eckhart Tolle*

Thoughts are the real determiners of Freedom. Forgiveness allows the old to pass away and the new to emerge as possibility. For in truth, we forgive ourselves; the perceived offender is the recipient of the Grace as well. Judgment and anger disrupt the soul's matrix, while patience and gentleness cultivate a moral individualist. Children have taught me how much they are like little ponies (and thoughts) whose tranquility is disrupted by any errant thought or emotion.

> *To live the creative life, we must*
> *lose our fear of being wrong.*
> *—Joseph Chilton Pearce*

TEMPERING OF THE SOUL

Patience and gentleness are the result of tempering the soul in the well of forgiveness. Passion forges the fire of desire, calling the soul to emerge, not in guilt or innocence, but in creativity and imagination. If you cook with an iron skillet, you know a temper is a good thing; *you just don't want to lose the temper.* The temper is a boundary that keeps food from sticking to its surface. The process is called seasoning, which not only requires heating and cooling the skillet, but also applying oil in the process. The process is analogous to strengthening or tempering the iron of our will. In the course of desires and passions, or heating and cooling, we create our own oil for the anointing of our spirits. Forgiveness forges a new soul-force to encounter a perceived evil in ourselves and in others. Evil establishes a threshold; a conundrum or a riddle, to challenge newly won soul forces to transform obstacles to an ever-finer perception, where the supersensible heart can shine like the sun.

CHAPTER 8

All Things Are New

Beauty is a manifestation of secret natural laws,
which otherwise would have been hidden from us forever.
—Wolfgang von Goethe

In 2000, I embarked on a pilgrimage of sorts. I traveled to England where I explored sacred sites, sat in a crop circle and visited Ruskin Mill, an institute for individuals with the diagnosis of Asperger's syndrome. Ruskin Mill was founded on the premise that modern life has robbed young people of the sensory and perceptual development they need to develop a healthy engagement with Life. Young children today are less inclined to explore three-dimensional space, and so the early movements of griping, rotating, sliding, lifting, and crawling are compromised. The therapy for this arrested development was seen in the performance of pre-Industrial Age arts and crafts. The theory behind this curriculum included the belief that when formative forces become engaged in ever denser and demanding creative processes, the individual can recapitulate missed stages of development. Through these archetypical movements, arrested development could be released towards further development. Forces below the threshold of consciousness could learn to learn. As the human being evolves, potential capacities that were previously uneducated begin to function, meeting the periphery in a more imaginative, creative, and human manner. Re-animating movement releases creative forces that were frozen in time or in a state of shock.

Students at Ruskin Mill worked outside 365 days of the year, rain or shine, tending sheep that were later shorn, the wool carded, spun, and then woven on looms operated by people; the looms were not powered by water or electricity. The resulting cloth was beautiful. Forestry required culling trees, using some for the charcoal that fired ceramic kilns or baker's ovens. The best timber was crafted into furniture by pulley driven, foot-powered devices. They raised vegetables and fish. There was a social component that connected the residents to their community for governance and celebration. The key ingredient was transparency in all the activities and that every community member was involved in all the aspects of communal life. Ruskin Mill was successful enough that the British government was interested in studying the community for its therapeutic success.

The mill was built on a small river in a valley that the students had transformed into gardens and pathways. While walking along a path through the gardens, I came across a sundial. This was no ordinary sundial. (See image.) What made it unique was that it charted the path of the sun through the year. At 51.5 degrees latitude, the sundial recorded the inscription of a circle in summer and one in the winter. Though only a speculation on my part, had this device been on the equator, the two circles would be nearly symmetrical to create a vesica piscis on any fixed place on the face of the earth throughout the course of the year. The implication of the sun's handiwork gave me pause and goosebumps. If this were so, then the vesica piscis is the signature of the sun.

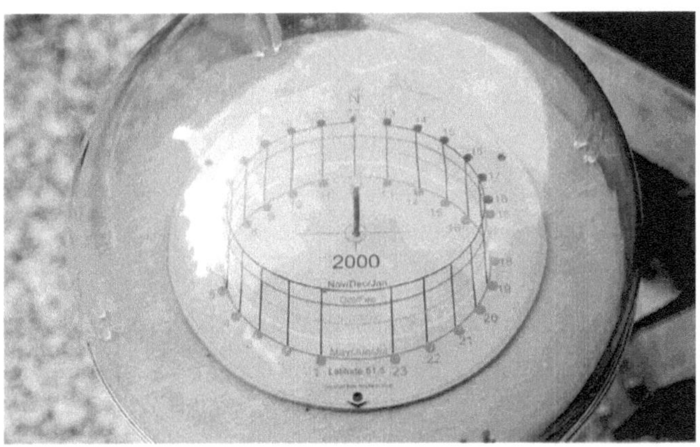

I left Ruskin Mill to travel south and west to arrive in Glastonbury, well known for its connection to King Arthur and the Holy Grail. The mystical island of Avalon was thought to have been just outside its city limits. King Arthur, with Guinevere at his feet, is supposed to be buried on the old abbey's grounds. Glastonbury is a premiere destination for all of us Grail seekers, and I'm no exception.

There are many myths and legends surrounding the Grail that Jesus blessed during the Last Supper. It was later thought to have held the blood of Christ from the crucifixion. There is a legend that Joseph of Arimethia brought the chalice to what is now Glastonbury, where he hid it in a well. This well and surrounding gardens are now a tourist attraction, of course. The waters from the well come from deep within the earth and are revered to have powers that have been and are used for baptisms and healing.

I followed the path that led to the Chalice Well where the Grail was once believed to have been hidden. The symbol of the vesica piscis in varying stages of perfection were represented along this path as circles of dissimilar sizes The actual chalice well is located at the farthest reaches of the garden and it is there that I found the most perfect representation of the vesica piscis on the wrought iron well cover. In 1919, Fredrick Bligh Bond designed the cover for the well and gave it to the Chalice Well Garden as an offering for peace. As I have written, this ancient symbol has been found throughout the world. But here at the well, piercing the vesica piscis was a lance as if holding the balance between the visible and invisible, conscious and unconscious, Masculine and Feminine worlds. The lance, or sword, is often construed to mean one's word or thinking that can pierce through the superficial to penetrate to the Truth. This sword has a double edge as if to warn of the danger of inflicting harm on the bearer as well; what you do to others is likewise done to you. Through this symbol, we can experience the connection between heaven and earth with the cross as the primary emerging form. Here in Glastonbury, the home of the Grail is a remarkable image to aspire to a life in balance that can lead to and through the sacred space, a Sacred Door.

The light of the body is the eye (I):
If therefore thine eye be single…
—Matthew 6:22

THY BODY WILL BE FULL OF LIGHT

Had it not been for Rudolf Steiner, the scientific work of Wolfgang von Goethe may have gone unnoticed. However, at an early age, Steiner was commissioned to translate Goethe's scientific work that describes metamorphosis, light, and color.

Steiner believed that Goethe's greatest inspiration to science was his study of metamorphosis. This commission inspired the founding thoughts for Anthroposophy, Steiner's gift for the serious seeker of revelation. Goethe's work, he believed, could inspire the student to an ever deeper appreciation of the wonders of the natural world, as Nature is infused through and through with the love and thoughts of the Creator. Steiner revered Goethe's scientific, yet poetically inspired, approach to Nature so much that the world headquarters for Anthroposophy in Switzerland is named the Goetheanum.

Goethe lived from August 28, 1747, to March 22, 1832, making him a contemporary of Thomas Jefferson, the economist Adam Smith, and the virtuoso Beethoven. These men were born on the cusp of emerging scientific thought of the Age of Reason that was devoted to order and crafted detail. On the other hand, we have another approach to Nature. We have a neoclassical devotion to observable phenomena with a striving for intuition and personal experience of the world. Goethe denied rationality's superiority as the "divine interpreter" of phenomena as his work required the observer to be the mediator and synthesizer of impressions. He not only made wonderful contributions to music, drama, poetry, and philosophy, but he believed he would be remembered most for his studies of color and light. He was strongly against Newton's analytical treatment of color, and though Goethe did not repudiate Newton's findings on the nature of light and color, he felt that Newton's theory was only part of a grander truth. Goethe was more captivated by how a phenomenon was perceived, and not how it was quantified. He believed that intuitive intelligence unites sense impressions to bring meaning similar to reading when symbols are linked to together to create meaning. Color is, in fact, the language of the soul.

Sir Isaac Newton was born 106 years before Goethe. He is still considered the greatest genius who ever lived, rivaled only by Albert Einstein. Newton was a multi-tasking genius who achieved recognition as a physicist, mathematician, astronomer, natural philosopher, alchemist, and theologian. He is credited for laying the foundation for classical mechanics and describing universal gravitation in the form of the three laws of motion that have affected scientific thought for over three centuries. He believed the universe was dynamically informed. Every school- aged child knows that he arrived at his revelation of gravity by watching an apple fall from a tree. He is credited with having proved a heliocentric universe. Surely, Copernicus and Galileo slept better in their graves. No doubt Newton was not only a scientific whiz, but he was also the first commoner to be entombed in Westminster Abbey in London, England.

I do not know what I may appear to the world,
but to myself I seem to have been only like a boy playing on the sea shore
and diverting myself now and then finding a smoother pebble or prettier shell
than ordinary whilst the great ocean of truth lay all undiscovered before me.
—Sir Isaac Newton

Both Newton and Goethe studied light and color, but came up with very different conclusions. Newton's empirical approach studied what happened when colorless white light passed through a prism resulting in an externally manifesting rainbow of color. He concluded in his work, Optiks, that all spectral color wove together to make colorless white light. His theory was based on the observation that a prism decomposed light into colors that form the visible spectrum.

He used a secondary lens to recompose the projected rainbow back into white light. He came to believe that darkness was the absence of light, nothingness really. This was fascinating work for the time as science was exciting minds into a more empirical approach to grasping the miraculous. When Newton died, Alexander Pope wrote his epitaph:

Nature and Nature's laws lay hid in night.
God said, "Let Newton be."
And all was Light.

Legend has it that Goethe was so inspired by Newton's work with the prism that he begged to borrow prisms. The busy man that he was, he got carried away with his many other projects and did not return the prisms in what was considered a timely manner. After several attempts to retrieve the property, a messenger came to Goethe's home to insist on their return. Goethe, in his haste, examined the prism by not allowing light to pass through the prism; instead, he looked within the prism. What he discovered set him on a path to what he considered his most important work. He reportedly commented that, "I am the only one who knows the truth in the difficult science of color." The difference was how the phenomenon was perceived by the observer; he studied observation and the physiological effects of color, and the effects of opposed color led him to create a symmetrically arranged color wheel, with blue and yellow, the representatives of light and dark, as the only two pure colors. His approach was not quantifiable and therefore did not exert an influence on the growing scientific thought of the time.

When Goethe looked into and through the prism, he saw that there were two distinct spectrums of color; one spectrum registered the cool blues and purples, and the other registered the warm reds, oranges, and yellows. This led him to hypothesize that darkness is not the absence of light, but the opposite of it. Light and darkness are interrelated, just as the north and south poles of a magnet. The interrelationship between dark and light creates the experience of color. Goethe concluded that color is a result of the two active principles of light and dark. He also wrote that Newton was incorrect to believe that darkness was a sort of nothingness. Goethe's experiment led him to write that darkness can weaken the light, and light can limit the energy of the dark, but in either situation, color arises. Yellow would be the result of diminished light, and blue is darkness under the influence of light.

What makes the two theories so different is that Newton insisted that all colors exist within white light and have no consequence outside of refraction. Goethe, on the other hand, observed that outside of light and darkness, when he looked through the prism onto a white wall, there was no rainbow at all. He concluded that there must be more to the phenomenon.

Goethe's color theory consists of experiments into the nature of color. He concluded that color results from the interaction of yellow and blue, the representatives of light and darkness and their attendant colors. He projected a focus in the prism until the two spectrums met, and the not- yet-included green arose. Goethe described this as the result of yearning of darkness toward the light-the darkness of blue yearning for the light of yellow. Color arises from the interplay of light and dark; darkness is something in itself and, as importantly, the observer has a subjective relationship to color. Color becomes an experience of subjectivity in the soul. Goethe's color work details the visual and moral effects of color. Color, he went on to speculate, is the feeling and language of the soul that reacts directly to impressions of what streams in through passive feeling.

THE MERMAID LOSES HER TAIL

Goethe continued his experiments and found that when the two spectrums were focused inwardly and brought together, the experience of duality vanished! In its place a magenta and viridian arose that do not exist in a spectrum of light; it did not exist in the unified outwardly manifesting rainbow.

The science of the day chose to use Newton's theory of light and color as building as a building block for optics. Goethe's work went unappreciated as it was considered a mere portrayal of light and not based in what science needed-facts. Steiner understood and said that in order to grasp Goethe's worldview, the aspiring initiate needed to develop the imagination, or organs of perception and intuition. Without engaging the imagination, observations are merely facts, and facts cannot bridge the threshold to behold the sacred. Goethe, a poet himself, would no doubt have agreed that imagination is a key to the door that unlocks the mysteries of the universe (uni-verse), where all is bound up in one glorious poem. He commented that, "Nothing is worse than imagination without taste."

Newton's rainbow is objectified in the bow of heaven that promises there is magic in the world. We understand its manifestation as a projection of light through droplets of water. When the sun shines from behind and through millions of water droplets, it produces the spectral colors of the rainbow. The angle of refraction is 40-42 degrees. This is marvelous to the imagination. Without a horizon to obscure it, the bow would manifest an enormous circle of color. The rainbow is a cone of color with the viewer at its apex. This is all good science. With Newton's theory of color, we can hypothesize that the viewer is, in fact, the gold at the end of the rainbow!

Do not all charms fly at the mere touch of cold philosophy?
There was an aw(e)ful rainbow once in heaven.
We know her woof, her texture, she is given-
In the dull catalogue of common things-
Philosophy will clip an Angel's wings,
Conquer all mysteries by rule and line,
Empty the haunted air and gnomed mine.
Unweave a rainbow.
-Sir Isaac Newton

Even with Newton's worldview, the whole can be greater than the sum of the particles. The imagination can take us into the realm of the invisible. By refining sensibilities at the periphery and strengthening one's focus, we create a spiritual gravity or magnetism that draws to one's self more and more of that self. When thinking and doing are in harmony within an individual, a supersensible heartbeat begins to throb. Living takes on a new dimension as the personal path appears and a door opens to the Field of Plenty. The vibrational matrix is the Universal Web of All Things.

There is only one journey. Going inside yourself.
-Rainer Maria Rilke

Goethe's work with what he called the sufferings and deeds of light directs the spiritual scientist inward to perceive that by understanding the value of both the light and the dark, one can focus the active properties of duality-male and female. The experimenter can move the material causing the split spectrum to come closer and closer until the duality vanishes, as it were, to create the projection of color through the prism, creating a viridian green where the two spectrums meet. When the two spectrums are further pressed together, duality, the experience of both poles, vanishes, and in its place two colors appear that did not previously exist. The viridian remains as a representative of the mediation between light and dark. As a companion to the viridian, magenta precipitates like dew as a new color.

Magenta is not a compromise; magenta is a metamorphosis, a solution to the overcoming of a previous limitation. Rudolf Steiner called this magenta the color of the human soul. If you were to shine a light through the darkness of your hand, the resulting color approaches this living color. The healing practices that use color look to magenta to stimulate and rebuild the heart, normalize blood pressure, depress veins or arteries toward normal functioning, and, as with green, make other colors more effective. A person must be steadfast to coax the magenta into partnership with the viridian.

Newtonian color theory disregards magenta as it does not appear as a spectral color. This, I believe, is yet another misunderstanding. If viridian appears as a yearning of darkness for the light, it is a product of the yellow and blue dynamic…a more masculine appearance. Magenta must therefore be generated from the reds and purples of the respective polarity. Magenta is created out of a higher frequency of color and more subtle perception allows for something new that has not appeared before, and a representative of the other polarity-the feminine.

The crucible of transformation takes place in the Third Space created by the polarity, the vesica piscis. It is a chrysalis of sorts. The butterfly is not formed by a committee representing both sides of the aisle. The resolution to growth does not rearrange the parts or shed a skin to allow something bigger to take form. The caterpillar passes through distinct phases, and when it enters the pupa stage, it secrets a hormone that liquefies the caterpillar. The caterpillar is transformed into another creature all together through a process called metamorphosis. Metamorphosis is a creative solution born out of Nature's laws.

In *'Finding Our Way Home'*, David Karten describes the future butterfly cells…The future butterfly cells are already distributed at different locations within the body of the caterpillar. These small clusters of tiny cells are called imaginal buds. They embody the blueprint of the butterfly. The immune system of the caterpillar recognizes them as foreign and tries to attack them, but the caterpillar does not try to "compete," and there is no battle for dominance. The imaginal buds absorb nutrients from the seeming puddle of ooze. The buds take on different body parts, cell attracts cell, and they cluster together. How sad the first awakening imaginal cell must be until it finds likeminded cells to create the butterfly. The caterpillar/butterfly is a single organism with the same genetic code. What appears as a powerful, devastating process in the caterpillar, transforms the caterpillar into a butterfly. The caterpillar literally disappears, leaving a mere impression of itself on the inside of the cocoon. The butterfly appears as if from far on the periphery as a solution to the limitation of the caterpillar's earthbound existence.

> *Artists hold two opposing views and still function.*
> —*F. Scott Fitzgerald*

CHRYSALIS, CROSS, AND CHRIST

Something operating on the periphery of our social organism is changing. The mermaid, as the evolving strengthening presence of the Feminine, is refining her sensibilities to join thought and deed, Masculine and Feminine, as the awakening that will facilitate a worldwide paradigm Shift. Perhaps her three hundred years of selfless service is up and she eagerly anticipates the transformation or metamorphosis of her soul. At the moment of transformation, the worldview is forever changed. She will lose her tail and be able to stand on her own two feet.

> *Once you become aware of this force for unity*
> *in life, you can't forget it.*
> *It becomes a part of everything you do.*
> *—John Coltrane*

The mystery of the Grail informs us that the color of the Grail is emerald green—viridian most likely. Filling it is the Elixir of Life, the magenta of the human soul. The vesica piscis is in fact symbolic of the *Holy Grail.* The Grail is not some illusory symbol for the unattainable. It is an image that ensures us that love and gratitude are guardians of a threshold of abundance. The devoted need not look further than their own being for the revelation that by healing senses to heal the soul, or healing the soul to heal the senses, a most miraculous event takes place. The middle path of experiencing Life is what transforms the soul, not some superstition of innocence. Nature herself is cheering us on.

By healing the senses and healing the soul we heal duality— but most importantly, we heal the split between the Masculine and Feminine. This is at the very foundation of modern life causes alienation within communities and sets country against country. There will be no peace until the virtues and qualities of compassion, forgiveness, and unconditional love are integrated into the evolutionary conversation. We are all connected, but we can only affect change by healing ourselves. The metamorphosis of soul into a vision of the vesica piscis creates a body that holds the Elixir of Life. So, by creating a "body" whether an individual, family, community, classroom, or nation, that can hold the human spirit, we are finding the Grail in our own backyards.

In a real sense, all life is interrelated.
All persons are caught in an inescapable network of
mutuality, tied in a single garment of destiny.
Whatever affects one directly, affects all indirectly.
I can never be what I ought to be and you can never be
what you ought to be until I am what I ought to be.
This is the interrelated structure of reality.
—Martin Luther King Jr.

Our society has reached a crisis of leadership brought about by poor thinking that creates misunderstanding and a lack of consciousness. The adversarial forces continue to press us into the realization that whether or not global warming is human-induced, we are the determiners of the course of history. We have been climbing an evolutionary mountain and are now close to the top where we are individually and collectively confronted by a storm. We find shelter and wait and wait for the storm to subside. We are marginally comfortable, but there is still a storm outside.

Another group of travelers arrives; the next morning, they make preparations to leave. The original party questions the decision to leave as quite obviously there is a storm raging outside the door. The departing party, knowing the mountain they are to climb, assures them that there is always a storm at the summit. Nature is a perfect system driven by the elemental life that is influenced by the emotions and thoughts of human beings. The Threshold is guarded with the intention of providing acknowledgment of the movement from one awareness to the next. By moving through the experience, even if death is the outcome, one becomes conversant with the powers of creation and resurrection. But better still is the grace of knowing process, new life, and the attendant presence of Love that directs the manifest.

The habit of ignoring our present moments
in favor of others yet to come
leads directly to a pervasive lack of awareness
of the web of life in which we are embedded.
—Jon Katat Zinn,

The world is one living organism. We are all not only connected in this web of life, but its survival is dependent on the stewardship of those of us who know that our thoughts travel, one to the other, like a whale's or mermaid's song on water. The song sets up channels of well-being that fuel the soul-life and creates the electrical matrix. Too many of us are comfortable enough, have money enough, or are pretty enough that we see no advantage in charging the matrix with our sacred intentions. The field weakens and brothers and sisters of all kingdoms fall through the web, unable to lend the potency of their becoming.

All that we do now must be done in
a sacred way and in celebration.
We are the ones we've been waiting for.
—Hopi Elder, Oraibi, Arizona

Drunvelo Melchizek's life's work has been devoted to the teachings of the Flower of Life. The Flower itself is a series of circles forming multiple vesica piscises, and contains within its proportions every single aspect of Life. It contains every harmony in music, everything that is within the waveform universe. This wisdom points to the viability and enormous potential of the Web of Life. Drunvelo Melchizek's teachings illustrate how the Flower has within its proportions the points to create all Platonic Solids. Platonic Solids form the foundation of all of Life. It is the language of Silence and the language of Life expressed through pure shape and proportion.

Not only do these ancient teachings illustrate the foundation of matter, but they also point to a diagram or blueprint of the connectivity of each person, one to the other. The laws that govern the emergence of the butterfly from out of the chrysalis are also the laws that guide and direct individual flowering. My favorite new word is *egregore*, which is both a noun and a verb. It describes an active ingredient in the group's mind. The meaning encompasses the notion that relationships create an energy that interacts and influences members of the group to help realize objectives. It can take on a life of its own, acting as a presence in the world. It can grow in strength, last for centuries, and be effective beyond the mere sum of its parts. Something marvelous is developing into the revelation that we are more than the sum of our parts. The Second Coming of Christ just might be in the community.

We live in a time of crisis and opportunity; a time when personal revelation is the only passage open to negotiate the physical world. Americans are born for personal revelation and revelation is like manna to artists. Artists are the new mystics and mystics can become the new revolutionaries.

The problems we face today may manifest around racial or political lines, but the real source of misery is a lack of understanding of the true nature of what it means to be a human. We are an ever-evolving, collective being, learning to redefine limitation. To this end, we may be tricked into believing we are different from our neighbors because of the way we appear on the surface. At the heart of the evolutionary crisis, we are learning to create a heart formed by individual catharsis, to nurture a soul, and to build a body that can hold spirit. The solutions to the problems we are facing begin with the individual and radiate out to build communities that include the welfare of all people.

Nature's premier community builders are the bees. The queen is created by a community of workers who feed her a sort of magical substance called royal jelly. The love for our work and artistic application creates a similar substance that is intended to be a communion of sorts for the community we serve. If the new frontier is within us and between us, then each person we meet is in fact a sort of royalty; a gate keeper to the future.

When we seek for connection, we restore the world to
wholeness. Our seemingly separate lives become meaningful
as we discover how truly necessary we are to each other.
Relationships are all there is. Everything in the universe
only exists because it is relationship to everything else.
Nothing exists in isolation.
—Margaret Wheatley

The question of whether or not I am my sister's keeper is rhetorical. What is true is that when I heal myself, I heal the world.

It's never too late to be what you might have been.
—George Eliot

Life's most urgent question is what are you doing for others.
—Martin Luther King Jr.

To see a world in a grain of sand,
and heaven in a wildflower,
hold infinity in the palm of your hand
and eternity in an hour
William Blake.

The new frontier is not in outer space. The frontier is in exploring thresholds of awareness that challenge each one of us every day to see our neighbor, see our world with new eyes. Thresholds are where the action is; borders become happenings of uncommon interest. There is a fascinating dynamic at work at a threshold. These are crossing points where the transitory can reveal the subtlety of the Divine at work in everyday occurrences. Behold all the things that can be made new.

"Give us this day our daily bread"
- Matthew 6:11

The inspiration I received from the mermaid is to examine a question from multiple directions, to see what revelation can be found by looking in and looking out. What does an issue look like backward? I drew the illustration of the recurring pentagram in the Preface by executing a pentagon. Within the primary pentagon, I created a pentagram by connecting the appropriate points. From the inner pentagram and the outer pentagon, I had the necessary point to continue indefinitely with ever-increasing dimensions. I first had to go in before I could go out to the pentagram and pentagon that could expand to the periphery. The effect illustrates how to look at one thing from many directions: big, tiny, right side up and upside down, inside out and outside in. The experience of arriving at perspective in this way approaches an alchemical process of decomposing and constructing a principle to arrive at essence. In the process, a perceived *evil* can be resurrected as *live*.

I was recently in a classroom where a poster hung on the wall that read: *Learn to create*. The phrase annoyed me; not in an obnoxious way, but as though something was not quite right about the wording. After a few days, the words rearranged themselves in my mind to read: *Create to learn*. Ahh! I felt relief.

We all feel something is not quite right in the political discourse of the world today. There is a voice missing that needs to be heard, but the job of making it right can appear daunting. The answers demand a new kind of thinking infused with love to be of service to make the world a better place. Not in Afghanistan, but in every neighborhood and community of hometown USA. An old paradigm is passing away and it is time to ask a question that couldn't be asked before.

What if we have only heard Adam's side of the creation story?

What if now is the moment in time when we choose to look deeper and listen better? Changing the flight of an arrow requires little to no change at all to make a big difference. Have courage, love, sing, celebrate, and pray. Make yourself interesting because no hand of the invisible will interfere unless invited.

Quotation References

I chose to include information about the people whose quotes I included in the book. I am pleased to note that they come from a wide range of disciplines and time periods. I tried to locate each reference, but, unfortunately, some names did not have a birth and death year or were too common and therefore, I was not able to identify all of them.

Agatha Christie *(1890–1976) was a British author who wrote short stories and crime novels. She, according to the Guinness Book of World Records in 2011, is considered the all time best-selling novelist.*

Albert Einstein *(1879–1955) was a Jewish/German genius. Many consider him to be the father of modern physics. He was visiting the United States when Hitler came to power, and he did not return to Germany. He denounced the using of nuclear power as a weapon. He is best known for his theory of relativity and E=mc2.*

Alexander Pope *(1646–1717) was an English poet who is remembered for his translations of Homer's The Iliad and The Odyssey.*

Aldous Huxley *(1894-1963) was a British writer of short stories and novels. He is best known for Brave New World. He was a humanist, pacifist, and satirist.*

Alfred, Lord Tennyson *(1809–1892) was poet laureate of the UK during Queen Victoria's reign. He was responsible for many phrases that now stand on their own like "…it is better to have loved and lost than never to have loved at all."*

Amanda Adams *(1976-) is a contemporary writer and archaeologist. Her work, The Mermaid's Tale, is a fusion of poetry and prose. She is also a fashion model.*

Ambrose Bierce *(1842–1913) was an American writer. He was one of thirteen siblings who all had names starting with "A," alphabetically according to their birth order.*

Anaïs Nin *(1903–1977) was of French and Cuban descent. She is remembered for the journals she wrote over the course of sixty years.*

Anne Morrow Lindbergh *(1906–2001) was the wife of Charles Lindbergh and a pilot herself.*

Annie Dillard *(1945——) is an American novelist, poet, and Pulitzer Prize winner.*

Audre Lorde *(1934–1992) was an African American poet, novelist, and essayist.*

Anne Cushman *is a contemporary American yoga instructor turned writer. She shares her life and spiritual awakenings in clever and witty prose.*

Antonio Machado *(1875–1939) Born Antonio Cipriano José Maria y Francisco de Santa Ana Machado y Ruiz; he was a Spanish poet.*

Artur Schnabel *(1882–1957) was Austrian by birth. He was highly respected as a musician and has been celebrated for his interpretations of Beethoven and Schubert.*

Aranyaka Sanskrit *word for part of the Hindu four Vedas from about 700 BC.*

Barbara DeAngelis *(1951—) American born, Barbara is a relationship consultant and professor at the Maharishi University of Management founded by Maharishi Mahesh Yogi.*

Bob Dylan *(1941—) An American musician, Bob Dylan was born Robert Allen Zimmerman. Dylan is a singer, songwriter, musician, and poet who become the voice of social unrest during the 1960s.*

Buckminster Fuller *(1895–1983) was an American engineer who coined terms like "Spaceship Earth" and "synergetics." He developed, among many other inventions, the geodesic dome.*

C. Lichtenberg *(1742–1799) was a German scientist who was the first to hold a professorship dedicated to experimental physics. His Lichtenberg figures are branching patterns created by high voltage discharges along surfaces or inside electrical insulators.*

C. S. Lewis *(1898–1963) His full name was Clive Staples Lewis, but he was known as Jack to those who loved him. He was an Irish writer of various disciplines. His works include The Chronicles of Narnia and The Screwtape Letters.*

Calvin Coolidge *(1872–1933) was the thirtieth president of the United States. He succeeded Warren G. Harding after Harding's death in 1923. One of Coolidge's biographers said that Coolidge embodied the hopes and dreams of the American middle class. He was a small government conservative.*

Carl Jung *(1875-1961) was Swiss and considered the father of modern psychology. He is best remembered for his contributions to understanding archetype, the collective unconscious, and synchronicity. His areas of interest include alchemy, astrology, and sociology.*

Carol Pearson *(1939—) is an American author, poet, screenwriter, and devout Mormon.*

Charles Franklin Kettering *(1876–1958) was the inventor of electrical ignition.*

Chechov *(1860-1904) was a Russian physician, dramatist and author. He said, "Medicine is my lawful wife and literature is my mistress." He felt that an author's role was to ask difficult questions, not to answer them.*

Chozan Shissai *was a Master Swordsman in the tradition of Zen Buddhism, an art practiced to attain enlightenment. He was born in Japan and lived in the 1700s.*

Christopher Fry *(1907–2005) was an English poet and playwright best known for The Lady's Not For Burning.*

Chuang Tzu *lived around the fourth century in China. He is considered the most renowned Taoist since Lao Tzu.*

Clarissa Pinkola Estes, PhD *(1945—) is a poet, Jungian psychoanalyst, and post trauma specialist. She studies the social and psychological patterns of cultural and tribal groups. She ministers to trauma victims including soldiers, prisoners, and the severely injured cast-away children. She has received numerous awards, including the Joseph Campbell Keeper of the Lore Award, and is highly respected as an agent of change on an international level.*

Constance Peter Cavafy *(1863–1933) was a well-known Greek poet. He examined aspects of Greek nationalism, homosexuality, and Eastern Orthodox Christianity.*

D.H. Lawrence *(1885–1930) used his talents as a novelist, poet, and painter to reflect on the dehumanizing effects of industrialization. He made many enemies and went into a voluntary exile that he called his savage pilgrimage. He lived to rise above his critics to be considered on of the greatest imaginative novelist of his generation.*

Dag Hammarskjöld *(1905–1961) was born in Germany and was a Secretary of the United Nations. He is the only person to receive the Nobel Peace Prize posthumously. He died in a plane crash on the way to a cease- fire negotiation.*

(the) Dalai Lama *(1935—) The name Dalai Lama is the Mongolian word for "ocean" and the Tibetan word for "leader." He is considered by his devotees to be the current incarnation of a long line of spiritual teachers.*

Dante Alighieri *(1265-1321) known as Dante, was an Italian poet, literary theorist, moral philosopher and political thinker. He is best remembered for his epic poem, the Divine Comedy.*

Ebnath Easwaran *(1910-1999) was born in the Kerala state of South India. He devised a method of meditation called Passage Mediations which asked the meditant to memorize inspirational passages from the world's great religions. He remembers his mother as someone who lived the example of spiritual practice.*

Edward Steichen *(1879-1973) was an American photographer, painter and art curator.*

Eckhart Tolle *(1948—) was born in Germany, but now lives in Canada. He is the author of A New Earth and The Power of Now. The New York Times named Tolle as the most spiritually influential person in the world.*

Eli Siegel *(1902–1978) was a Latvian immigrant to the United States. He was the founder of aesthetic realism. "All beauty is the making one of the permanent opposites in reality."*

Elie Wiesel *(1928—) won the 1986 Nobel Peace Prize.*

Elizabeth Barrett Browning *(1806–1861) was a prominent Victorian poet.*

Emily Dickinson *(1830–1886) was a very private poet who was not truly appreciated until after her death. She is now considered a major poet.*

Etty Hillesum *(1914–1943) was a Polish Jew who kept a diary during the German occupation of Amsterdam. She repeatedly turned down opportunities to go into hiding and said that she wanted to "share her people's fate."*

Eric Maisel *is a contemporary American writer who wrote books like: Mastering Creative Anxiety and Fearless Creating.*

F. Scott Fitzgerald *(1896–1940) is considered one of the greatest American authors of the twentieth century.*

Francis Bacon *(1561–1626) was a man of many interests including philosophy, law, and science. He was influential as an advocate of the scientific method at the time of the scientific revolution.*

Fredich Nietzche *(1844-1900) was a German philosopher who challenged many Christian premises. He valued life, creativity, and power. He was an Existentialist. His questioning of prevalent values and morality of his time inspired many creative people to explore their own motivations.*

Friedrich Schiller *(1759–1805) was a German poet and philosopher*

Fyodor Dostoyevsky *(1821–1881) was a Russian author who wrote Crime and Punishment and The Brothers Karamazov. His work examined how human beings behave during difficult political and social times.*

Galway Kinnell *(1927—) is a poet and the author of Mortal Acts, Mortal Words.*

George Eliot *(1819-1880) was a pseudonym for Mary Anne Evans. She was an English novelist, journalist and translator of the Victorian era. She wrote seven novels, but used a masculine pen name because she felt she would be taken more seriously as a man.*

George MacDonald *(1824–1905) was a Scottish minister best known for fairy tales. He wrote Princess and the Goblin, The Golden Key and Phantastes. He inspired Madeleine L'Engle, Tolkein, and C.S. Lewis.*

Giordano Bruno *(1548-1600) was an Italian philosopher.*

H.P. Blavasky *(1831-1891) Born Helena Petrova, Blavasky was a Russian mystic who founded the Theosophical Society, an organization for universal brotherhood.*

Hafiz *was a Sufi mystic.*

Harriet Beecher Stowe *(1811–1896) was an American abolitionist and author of Uncle Tom's Cabin. The book galvanized the anti-slavery movement while angering many people in the South.*

Henry Kissinger *(1923—) is a German-born American who was Secretary of State under Richard Nixon and Gerald Ford.*

Henry David Thoreau *(1817–1862) was an American activist, author, and naturalist. He was an environmentalist before there was even an environmental movement. He is best known for Walden Pond, a Life in the Woods.*

(Sir) Isaac Newton *(1642–1727) was a Renaissance man of great scope. He and Albert Einstein are considered to have been the greatest scientific minds of all time.*

J.J. Van der Leeuw *is a modern day Theosophist.*

Jack Kornfield *(1945—) After graduating from college in 1967, Kornfield joined the Peace Corps. He spent time in Thailand where he met Ajahu Chah, a Buddhist teacher of meditation. He is a prolific and well- respected author. His work is shaped by Eastern spiritual teachings, but designed for a Western audience.*

Jean Anouih *(1910–1987) was a French dramatist whose work explored issues of integrity in a world of moral compromise.*

(Sir) John Betjemen *(1906–1984) was an English poet, writer, and broadcaster who called himself a "poet and a hack." He was a UK poet laureate.*

John Boormen *(1933-) is a British film maker known for Point Blank, Tailor of Panama, and Excalibur.*

John Coltrane *(1926-1967) was an American jazz musician. He felt that all a musician can do is to get closer to the sources of nature, and so feel that he is in communion with the natural laws. He was awarded the Pulitzer Prize Special Citation for masterful improvisation.*

John Donne *(1572–1631) is considered the preeminent representative of metaphysical poets.*

John Keats *(1758–1821) was a Romantic poet and contemporary of Lord Byron. He became more famous after his death and is now considered one of England's most beloved poets.*

John Muir *(1838–1914) was an American naturalist and advocate for the preservation of wilderness. He founded the Sierra Club.*

Jon Kabat Zinn *(1944—) His studies with Zen Master Seung Sahn have influenced his medical career, as he has integrated Eastern and Western science into his practice. He teaches mindfulness meditation.*

Joseph Chilton Pierce *(1926—) His writings focus on the idea of the heart or compassionate mind. He believed imaginative play to be the most important activity for the young child. His books include The Crack in the Cosmic Egg, Spiritual Initiation and the Breakthrough of Consciousness: the Bond of Power, and A Return to the Intelligence of the Heart.*

Joseph Murphy *(1898–1981) was born a Catholic in Ireland, but after an experience with healing prayer, he moved to the United States, where he met Emmet Fox and Ernest Holmes who introduced him to Religious Science. As a minister, he built the Los Angeles Divine Science Church into one of the largest New Thought congregations in the country.*

Julia Cameron *(1948—) is the author of The Artist's Way.*

Kahil Gibran *(1883–1931) was a Lebanese-American poet known mostly for The Prophet, an inspirational book. He is the third bestselling poet, behind Shakespeare and Lao Tzu.*

Katherine Mansfield *(1883–1923) was born in New Zealand, but lived in England, where she became friends with D.H. Lawrence and Virginia Woolf. She contracted tuberculosis and died before she could return to New Zealand.*

Lauren Thatcher *Ulich (1938—) is a historian of early American women . Her work has been characterized as "the silent work of ordinary people."*

Leonard Cohen *(1934—) Canadian by birth, Leonard Cohen is a singer, songwriter, poet, and novelist. He spent many years in a Zen Buddhist monastery.*

Lily Tomlin *(1939—) She is an American comedian appreciated for her improvisation.*

Maalidoma Patrice Somé *(1956—) was born in West Africa. He was kidnapped by Jesuit missionaries at the tender age of four years old. When he was twenty, he ran away and underwent an arduous initiation process to reenter the society of his birth, the Dagara. The Dagara give each person a name that reflects their unique destiny. Maalidoma means, "become friends with the stranger/enemy." He is now a respected professor in the United States.*

Madeleine L'Engle *(1918–2007) was well loved for her young adult fiction. Her work is a reflection of her curiosity about science and Christianity.*

Margaret Mead *(1901–1978) was an American cultural anthropologist. Her work on attitudes toward sex in the South Pacific and Southeast Asia influenced the sexual revolution in the 1960s.*

Margaret Wheatley *Is alive today, but I could not find a record of her birth year. (Timeless) She has worked all over the earth and in virtually every type of organization. She studies organizational behaviors.*

Margery Williams *(1881–1944) was an English/American writer of popular children's books. She is best remembered for The Velveteen Rabbit.*

Marie Ebner-Eschenbach *(1830–1916) was an Austrian novelist. She coined the phrase "even a stopped clock is right twice a day."*

Marilyn Ferguson *(1938-2008) was an American author, editor and public speaker who is best known for her book, Aquarian Conspiracy,*

Martin Luther King Jr. *(1929–1968) was an American Baptist minister and leader of the African American civil rights movement. He was a proponent of nonviolence in the tradition of Mahatma Gandhi, and he was the youngest person to receive the Nobel Peace Prize. He was assassinated on April 4, 1968.*

Masau Emoto *(1943—) is the author of Message from Water. Emoto is of Japanese descent and has gained notoriety for his research concerning the effects of human consciousness on water at the molecular level.*

Morris Mandel *(1911–2009) was born in Poland, but he moved to the United States. He was socially productive as a school counselor, teacher, and author of over fifty books.*

Novalis *(1772–1801) was a pseudonym for Georg Philipp Freiherr von Hardenberg, who was a philosopher and author in the German Romantic period.*

Oralibi *was an American Indian and Hopi elder.*

P.L. Travers *(1899–1996) Pamela Lyndon Travers was an Australian novelist best known for her children's series, Mary Poppins.*

Percy Shelley *(1792–1822) was a prominent English romantic poet and considered on of the best lyric poets.*

Phillippa Gregory *(1954—) is English, but was born in Kenya. She writes historical fiction and runs a small charity that builds wells in school gardens in Gambia.*

Pierre Simon de Laplace *(1749-1827) French astronomer and mathematician.*

Pierre Teilhard de Chardan *(1881–1955) was a French philosopher and Jesuit priest. Several of his books were censured by the Catholic Church. He believed in an ideal spirituality that transcends the physical and is realized through individual intuition rather than doctrines of established religion.*

Plato *(423–347 BC) was a classical Greek philosopher and student of Socrates. Aristotle was his student. These three men lay the foundation of Western philosophy.*

Pogo *was the lead character in an American comic strip created by Walt Kelly (1913–1973). The strip was satirical, funny, and political.*

Rabindianath Tagore *(1861-1941) was an East Indian poet who won the Nobel Peace prize for literature in 1913. He was a devoted friend of Gandhi.*

Rainer Maria Rilke *(1875–1926) was a poet born in Prague.*

Ralph Waldo Emerson *(1803—1882) was a uniquely American individualist who led the Transcendental movement. He delivered the speech, "The American Scholar," in 1837, which was considered an intellectual declaration of independence.*

Robert Collier *(1885–1950) was one of the first writers of self-help books. He wrote about topics that interest those of us on the path to a greater experience of Life.*

Robert Frost *(1874–1963) was an American poet who received four Pulitzer Prizes for his poetry.*

Robert Louis Stevenson *(1850–1894) was a Scottish writer, best known for Treasure Island.*

Rudolf Steiner *(1861–1925) was an Austrian who founded the Anthroposophical Society, an esoteric philosophy growing out of European Transcendentalism. He taught that thinking was no more or less an organ of perception than the eye or ear.*

Rumi *(1207-1273) was a mystic Sufi poet who wrote during the Persian Renaissance. His poetry can be characterized as that of a lover longing for union with the beloved.*

Salvador Dalí *(1904–1989) was a Spanish surrealist painter.*

Sam Keen *(contemporary to 2012) is a modern philosopher, professor, and author who explores subjects regarding love, religion, life, and what it is to be a man in contemporary society.*

Starhawk *(1951—) is the most popular voice for ecofeminism and is known for her theories of Paganism.*

Friedrich Schiller *(1759–1805) was a German poet.*

Sri Aurobindo *(1872–1950) was an East Indian nationalist and freedom fighter, fighting to end British domination. He was also a philosopher, yogi, and poet. "The spirit will look through Matter's gaze and Matter shall reveal spirit's face."*

T.S. Eliot *(1888–1965) was born American, but naturalized as a British subject at the age of twenty-five. He became known as the most important English language poet of the twentieth century.*

The Talmud is Hebrew*, meaning to teach or to study. It is the central text of mainstream Judaism and contains rabbinic discussions.*

Tan Guangzhen *was a Chinese philosopher.*

Timothy Leary *(1920–1996) was an American psychologist and writer who advocated the therapeutic benefits of psychedelic drugs. He coined the phrase, "turn on, tune in, drop out." President Nixon thought him to be "the most dangerous man in America."*

Victor Borge *(1909-2000) was a Danish comedian, conductor and pianist. He is playfully remembered as The Clown Prince of Denmark.*

Victor Hugo *(1802–1885) was a French writer best remembered for Les Miserables and The Hunchback of Notre Dame.*

W. Somerset Maugham *(1874–1965) was perhaps the highest paid English author of the 1930s.*

William Blake *(1757-1827) was an English poet, painter and printmaker during the Romantic Age. Although he was generally* *overlooked during his lifetime, he is remembered as one who embraced the imagination of God and the human being.*

Warren Buffet *(1930—) is an American investor and philanthropist, and perhaps the most successful investor in the world. In 2011, he was ranked the third wealthiest man in the world. He has pledged to give away 99 percent of his wealth.*

William Pitt *(1759–1806) was, at twenty-four, England's youngest Prime Minister, even before it the office was called Prime Minister.*

Wolfgang von Goethe *(1749–1832) was a German genius, scientist, poet, and writer, best known for his play, Faust.*

Zohar *is a mystical Jewish text.*

Acknowledgements

I would like to acknowledge the following resources. Each reference helped to clarify my thinking so that I could relate my thoughts through great thinkers and tinkers of the world. A special thanks to Wikipedia for providing fine biographical details that may have otherwise been overlooked.

The content of the book may not be Rudolf Steiner's philosophy, but it is a direct result of my work with Waldorf Education and Anthroposophy. The physics experiments I used to illuminate the text are not necessarily found in a specific book, but were passed on to me by mentors and colleagues.

References

Chapter One

Emoto, Masau Message from Water, Beyond Words Pub Co, ISBN 1582701148, 2004

Grimm's Fairy Tales, Pantheon Books, New York ISBN 0-394-49414- 6 1944/1972 The Goose Girl, and Briar Rose are tales that I have loved and learned from over a good many years. Even though I have taken the liberty to add my twist and turns to the retelling, I do not think I have diminished either story.

Spock, Marjorie , Fairy Worlds and Workers, St. George Publications, Spring Valley, New York ISBN 0-916786-3 1980

Scientific America, "Lightning between Earth and Space," p. 57 Stephen B. Mende, Davis D. Sentman, and Eugene M. Wescott 1997

Sussman, Linda. Speech of the Grail. Lindisfarne Books, United States ISBN-0-940262-69-X. 1995

www.ucla.edu/chlandi

Understandably, I have had a request to publish the full version of T.S. Elliots' poem, The Still Point. Here it is in its entirety for those who would enjoy it to its fullest:

The Still Point
by T.S. Elliot

*At the still point of the turning world . Neither flesh nor fleshless;
Neither from nor towards; at the still point, there the dance is, But
neither arrest nor movement. And do not call it fixity,
Where past and future are gathered. Neither movement from nor
towards, Neither ascent no decline. Except for the point, the still point,
There would be no dance, and there is only the dance.
I can only say, there have been: but I cannot say where. And I cannot
say, how long, for that is to place it in time,
The inner freedom from the practical desire,
The release from action and suffering, release from the inner And outer
compulsion, yet surrounded
By a grace of sense, a white light still and moving.*

Chapter Two

*Adams, Amanda,A Mermaid's Tale. Greystone Books. Vancouver/
Toronto/Berkley ISBN-13:978-55365-117-8 — ISBN-10:1-55365-
117-0.*

*2006. Her work is sheer poetry as she identifies herself with our mystical
creature, the mermaid.*

*Gregory, Phillipa. The White Queen.A Touchstone Book, Simon
&Schuster, ISBN 978-1-4165-6369-3 2009*

*MacDonald, George. Phantastes. Wm. B. Eerdmans Publishing
Company. Michigan. ISBN 0-8028-6060-5.*

*Osborne, Mary Pope, Mermaid Tales from Around the World. Scholastic
Inc., USA, ISBN 0-439-04781-1, 1993*

Rosen, Brenda. Mermaid Wisdom, Enrich Your Life with Insights from the Deep. A Godsfield Book. ISN-13: 978-1-84181-311-0, ISBN-10:1- 884181- 311-7. UK, 2006

Tarico, Valerie, "Trusting Doubt: a Former Evangelical Looks at Old Beliefs in a New Light." Psychologist and writer, Seattle, Washington. Founder of Wisdom Commons.

Schneider, Michael S, Beginner's Guide to Constructing the Universe. HarperCollins Publishers. New York. ISBN -06-016939-7. 1995.

The Bible and various holy texts have inspired me to write The Mermaid's Tale. Learning to think for myself has made all the various text new with remarkably the same message.

Travers, R.L. Parabola-Summer 1991 "Remembering." p.84 P.L. Travers ISBN 0362-1596

Steiner, Rudolf, Knowledge of Higher Worlds and How to Attain Them Anthroposophical Press ISBN 088010046X 1947

Chapter Three

www.northstar.com/mermaid www.msnbc.com/id/42154769/ns/ www. godandscience.org

Chapter Five

Pert, Candace, Molecules of Emotion, Scribner, ISBN 068484634 1999

Chapter Six

Hutchins, Eileen, Observation, Thinking, the Senses, Saint George Imprints, Spring Valley, New York, 1975

Mac Donald, George Phantastes, Wm. B. Eerdmans Publishing Co. first published 1858, republished 2000.

Chapter Seven

Abbott, Jacob, Light, Harper and Brothers, 1871,

Melchidek,Drunvalo, The Ancient Secret of the Flower of Life volume I and II, Light Technology Publishing 2000, ISBN 1-891824-21-X

About the Author

The Mermaid's Tale, in part memoir, draws on Sophia's 30-plus years in the classroom, but most notably 20 years she spent as a Waldorf teacher. Waldorf schools are inspired by the work of Rudolf Steiner, an Austrian visionary, whose insights into the evolution of consciousness of Western culture created a body of work known as Anthroposophy. This movement for spiritual renewal redefines not only education, but also agriculture and medicine. Humanity as a whole cannot move forward without addressing what it means to be a human being and what our relationship is to the Earth. Sophia has come to believe that a connection to the questions of love and morality is key to our collective survival.

Sophia and her life partner of 30 years live on 10 acres on the Ozark plateau in Missouri. She enjoys carving gourds and caring for their golden doodle, Dixie, and their tortie cat, Maple. Aside from her favorite pastime of riding her black mare, Katie, she loves porch sitting and playing cards with her girlfriends.

The gourd is 30 inches tall. I grew it myself.
Here is a description of her role in the Far East.

Contrary to Saint George. The Dragon Slayer of the West,
Quan Yin tames the dragon through compassion.

Legend has it that she not only tames the dragon
but rides astride this mighty beast.

She knows every dragon guards a mystery and that
seven heads grow back from a severed head.

Here we see her upon a lotus flower that has risen from the deep.

She holds a vial of human tears and in her
right hand is a pearl of great wisdom.

Flying above is the Phoenix risen from its own ashes.
Beauty for Ashes

Thank you, Lanie